Licorice

Licorice

by Bridget Penney

Book Works

Licorice

Angie dreams she is in the windmill. Creaking,
swaying, like a ship at sea: the building groans as its
sweeps catch the full force of the gale. Wood. Slats.
The grinding querns with their empty grooved
surfaces. Ladder reaching up to the top floor, another
going down. She wouldn't trust herself to those rungs.
Everything is shaking and wobbling. She's staying
where she is. She could lie down on the stones but she
knows better. I'm not grinding up my bones to make
anyone's bread. Laughter. What a daft idea. Her
mother's voice then Angie Angie come on out of there.
It's time to stop hiding. We have to go home. Digital
clock radio, crack of light between the curtains.
Rolling half over in the double bed, ghost of lavender-
scented pillow, her arm reaching out for Roy before
she remembers he isn't there. She stares at his side
of the bed. No smell of him, no stray hairs, she's
washed the sheets since he left good riddance really.
Shit. She tries to rub the sleep out of her eyes, throat
full of phlegm, cough, hope it's not raining again
today it's going to be really funny if we all end up with
double pneumonia

Thank fuck the weather is better today though the
light is still shit, everything cast under heavy lowering cloud. Aren't you used to that where you come
from? That's why I moved. Atmospheric enough well
sure just not the right kind of atmosphere: I want to
shoot this grisly tale of infanticide and cannibalism
in brilliant sunlight. It's August after all is that
so unreasonable? Bet it'll rain later. Well hurry up

move your arse out of there I've made you some coffee. I couldn't sleep last night your sofa springs were sticking in everywhere. I ended up on the floor aches and pains all over. Do you a favour and that's all the thanks I get. Just thought that, didn't say it. Got to keep on the right side of my leading man. Breakfast'll sort you out how about scrambled eggs on toast? Oh my god. Roy covers his face with his hands. Cereal with a non-dairy alternative if you have it. Don't want my skin erupting. You reckon medieval peasants had flawless skin? Talk to Licorice. I'll see what I can find in the downstairs kitchen. Licorice might have some

Angela Allardyce, twenty-four, 5ft 7inches, hair brown, eyes grey, experience in student films and as an extra in mainstream productions, has worked as a waitress, barkeep, in a hospital laundry that was the pits. She left her last job in retail before they could find out she'd been nicking stuff. Met Roy in a club and you know when something's a bad idea right way too full of himself but somehow we still ended up shagging on the beach and then I let him move in. Through him I met Pete and Licorice and got involved in their bloody film. She stomped up the track. Slippery film on the chalk rain has washed the grass white. It isn't even a windmill I keep saying, just someone's house they've sneaked through planning permission by making it look like one. We've knocked and knocked and Pete's put so many notes through the door but no one ever answers him. It's August. They're away. Oh shame you didn't contact them earlier of course they'd have said you can use our house

for your horror film while we're away on our hols.
It's not like we're asking to shoot there. Licorice puts
tiny squares of folded paper through the letter box
she showed me one and I said gosh that's beautiful
what have you drawn oh dear she laughed evidently I
haven't done a very good job but she posted it anyway
shrugging maybe it'll intrigue whoever picks it up
and they'll give me a ring

Speak land. Speak signposts. Speak ancient track
threading over the Downs, contoured by feet of men
and women horses cattle donkeys sheep and the
bellies of snakes. Grass snake or adder, interrupted,
black and white diamonds flash or pure black,
melanistic morph, but you can always tell a grass
snake by the mark behind its head. Looking up
at the sky the sun skiffs the clouds like a boat on the
fucking sea back down to earth and Pete thinks no
one has noticed the way he's looking at Angie. Angie
frowns and drops back behind the rest of us like
she can't really be bothered. She's wearing a bright
blue fleece and skinny jeans and carries a furled
umbrella in her left hand. Roy is quieter today he's
stopped protesting my smoking ban on location.
Nicorette up his arm. It's not just that I don't like it
this is the fourteenth century we're trying to recreate
and cigarettes are a fire risk, at least they will be if
ever the grass dries out. Pete hollers to stop and wait
for Angie. Can you sit down on the grass Ange? It's
wet. Have a plastic bag. I wanna see how you'll look
in that shot. This is before anything at all happens
you're just a young girl think those kind of young girl
thoughts. What the fuck do you think those are?

I have literally no idea which is why I'm asking you to do it. I'd rather Licorice directed me. Licorice what are you doing over there? Making notes on the script arsehole no I didn't say that. They didn't have no hedgerows back then I'm thinking Pete. Don't plan the shot here. Okay we'll shoot further up. What the fuck? You want me to climb? We're showing you as a free spirit. Angie my dear. Oh just get lost why don't you

It's my fucking script, after all. This is how it begins. Nan is doing chores for her mother, would have liked to have her fetching water from the well but we'd have had to find a wooden bucket and if there are any that haven't been repurposed as planters they're going to be full of holes. Everyone says Licorice you're such a stickler for textures but if you don't have the right textures how are you going to make the audience feel what you're trying to say? Nan could be collecting firewood instead plenty of brush we can cut with secateurs not too many brambles she moaned at first but give her a cloak made out of some old burlap sack now she's more into the idea. We will shoot close-ups of her carrying the sticks under her arm and her feet will be bare I'd walk her route myself with no shoes to be sure there is nothing that could injure her and she will be humming to herself then her mum's voice will cut in, yelling at her to hurry up. I'll play her mum my accent isn't that noticeable Pete offered to go falsetto but I didn't want her sounding like a pantomime dame. When Nan hears her mum's voice she just drops her bundle of wood and runs off up the hill. Early in the morning we'll film this and Roy

because he hasn't come into her life yet has the job
of being charming and persuading dog walkers and
runners to keep out of shot. And if they ask what's
the film about we say a local legend but not too many
people have heard of Nan Kemp though one old boy
did say there was a band of that name when he was
young and for all of two seconds I thought if we could
use their music but the sound design for what we
want will be much better served by the microphones
hanging up in the windmill so hold on for that if we
can get permission a day's recording should provide
enough rattles and squeaks to multitrack. It's far
enough away from the road that it won't pick up traffic noise and the voices of hikers if they stop to pet
the ponies won't go amiss

Anyway Ange in some kind of peasant dress I think
I've got that sorted, no cotton, I was particular about
that, has to be wool or linen. Linen, she said, because
wool is too hot and itchy but it's not linen as she's
thinking a cool summer frock or pair of elegantly
crumpled trousers. I suggested we made her a dress
out of nettles and explained that nettles yield fibres
akin to flax which can be spun, but she just said I
don't think you're going to get anyone to do that unless
you do it yourself and I agreed with her, I laughed
and said I wouldn't put you in a dress of nettles if
it was going to be prickly and yes probably what
I'll do is find some linen stuff in a charity shop and
fake it up. Sludgy cream colour or brown, what do
you think. Oh just something that blends me with
the landscape. That bad eh. It's those boys Licorice
they get me down. No she didn't say that. I waited

for anything else that might be forthcoming but she just said I hope you don't mind me asking and please say if you do but I've never met anyone called Licorice before I never even thought of it being a name. I don't mind you asking at all I said. If I divulge then perhaps she will tell me what went on with Roy and I'll find out if she notices the way Pete is looking at her now. Roy is fucking furious about it but he's not going to say anything to Pete because Pete's the director ha ha and anyway he's sleeping on his floor and I hope he doesn't say anything to Pete because Pete would make some unbearable remark about Ange not being Roy's girlfriend any longer and then Roy would ask if he could stay with me and I really don't want him around, as an actor he looks the part at least untidied a bit but as a human being I can't stand him. Whenever I direct him he's always tuned to what Pete is going to say next and it's fucking irritating

Licorice well now I do love Licorice. So many varieties, salty and sweet and chewy and satisfying. A lot of English people can't pronounce my name. It does sound a bit like Licorice so my first room mate she started calling me that. I found I didn't mind you know I was eighteen years of age and in a foreign country and it helped me blend in, at the same time everyone always remembered my name. It's really cool, Angie said, as long as you're okay with it. Now you tell me Angie, if you had to name yourself after a sweet what would you choose? That's a tough one! I don't know what do I like? Toffee apple? Toffee baaad apple. Sounds like a reject from The Factory. Sherbet maybe not that I like it all that much it

used to make me sneeze yeah sherbet fountain how's
that for a name ha ha. She made a funny face when
she stopped laughing. Embarrassed maybe and she
was thinking about sherbet fountains and licorice
and how all sherbet fountains had a piece of licorice
inside of them but for either of us to mention that
would have — would it have? made it sound like we
were coming on to each other and she was straight,
no question, she was just really fed up with the boys
and whatever she thought about me, I, unlike the
boys, wasn't wanting to sleep with her. I just want
her to be in my film she is fucking perfect. Skin like
milk, not pasty from sitting indoors over a screen
all day and night but looking like it's made from the
English weather, clouds and fog and dew like that
song, little lines of discontent around her eyes and
mouth and cropped hair growing through brown with
the ends still blonde where one day she got fed up
and had it all chopped off. Roy hates it I can tell he's
remembering the long blonde tresses he would screw
his hands into while she blew him. He's thinking she
did it just to spite him Pete however complimented
her new look and really, she answered with the
magnificent gravitas of unconcern, I'm surprised
you noticed. Would have been passive aggressive if
she cared a fig for Pete's opinion but, as it was, Pete
has the skin of a rhinoceros. It sticks up when she
twists her fingers through it and looks unfinished
sometimes like the whole of her head is aflame. Low
evening sun no clouds rifting deep shadows. Suits
her better. Or easily fixed with a wig we could go
raven what do you think if it doesn't make me look
too gothy? Nan in her off-white shift raised bare arms

cheap synthetic wig flopping around as she calls
down the elements on bloody everything. Her mum
her husband those babies she never wanted to have.
Toes digging into the earth heels slipping on that
soapy soapy chalk film molecules suspended in water
so everything just moves, lubricant between our feet
and the ground sends us sliding everywhere. It's
going in my eyes and mouth. I hate this wig. So glad
you said that because the texture's all wrong. Just
do it as you are. We're not looking for a wet T-shirt
moment here Pete. The past that we're trying to
capture is not that idea. It's a disgusting grisly piece
of history if it is history can you believe it really
happened. We don't need to believe having the story
is enough. We don't even know if Nan really existed,
this place is named for her, there used to be a sign,
I don't know what happened to it. It looked pretty
rotten even years and years ago probably just fell down
and someone broke it up and fed it to their wood-
burner. Like back before people would say to me
Licorice you've had that website up about your film
for two years what's going on. Not much ha ha ha
still chasing funding

Do you think Nan is really buried under the crossroads? How deep down? In pure chalk would it be
there in a white chamber studded with flints. She
wouldn't have been buried with any keepsakes or
grave goods. Sewed up in a sack as small as possible,
her head distracted from neck and torso by the
fracture of her upper cervical spine, and chucked
in. Trampled down. Chalk degrades bones and
makes them fragile relatively quickly. Kind of not

what I'd expect you think acid soil would be more aggressively damaging but there's all kinds of other factors coming into play, temperature, wetness, salt. We're near enough the sea to taste it when it rains. Calcium in bones has an affinity with calcium in chalk, after all chalk is made of all the tiny skeletons of past sea creatures, compacted into a brittle white block. And if Nan's bones have entirely disappeared she's part of the ground now. Nothing to find. The ground level has risen since then to be sure. More than by the tarmacking of the road when did that happen probably last century been redone a few times since the weight of cars as they roll along too fast necessitating it even if we never experience a hard frost. The road would have been white before then, deeply bitten by cart wheels. Slippery as fuck. Suicides were buried at crossroads to confuse their restless souls and stop them from wandering so why not a murderer too. This is where she endured the rough justice of her outraged community. Hanged from a big old tree for her terrible crime. Would she have been buried with a stake through her heart has someone watched too many horror films

Spindle berries are toxic hot pink mini-reticules dangling off bare twigs and if you split them open bright orange seeds are revealed. Then there are the juicy red slightly flattened hawthorn berries hawthorn candy yum you could make a ton of it but if the berries weren't here the whole land would be browner and whiter and duller. Licorice collects hawthorn leaves she says are different shapes, turning them over in her palm to fit the mismatched lobes together like

you're doing a tangram. A *tanagram*. I absolutely love
that idea. Most frequently occurring species along
the track is the wayfaring tree, sporting red and black
berries together that look luscious but are poisonous
to humans. Such a false friend: its fluffy white
umbels resemble elder but have none of the heady
scent that hits the back of your throat and its wood
won't burn unless you bung it on a fire that's already
blazing. We were shivering in the rain eating cold
soup the day Licorice forgot the fuel for her Trangia.
Then there are sloes, blackthorns with a sheeny
frost on their dark fruit and their bigger cousin the
damascene, everyone is out after them never managed to pick enough to make anything. Angie brought
a bottle of sloe gin. It's an acquired taste. Those who
likes their gin dry won't like it. Did you pick the
sloes yourself Ange. Naw Pete I didnae. Ah bought
it at the offie. Roy's watching me; he's pleased I
put Pete down the arrogant Scottish cunt. Look at
him next to Roy even if handsome is as handsome
does. *I* gave Roy that fine gold chain but before we
were done I wanted to strangle him with it for being
such a lying fuck. Those gold links would just have
burst apart up on the Downs scattered like treasure
for future archaeologists digging up their grave
goods not that there's any at all left. Licorice says
the Victorians thought giants were buried in these
barrows. Great tall skeletons, every bone longer than
people expected, mighty weapons beside them, did
that mean people thought that they had shrunk from
days of yore and when did they think the skeletons
were from was that when they started to imagine
prehistorical time?! But perhaps they just got the

bones muddled up it's not like if someone showed me a human bone I'd be able to identify which part of the body it comes from which is bizarre when I've got them all inside of me. Could I tell a humerus from a femur a scapula from my pelvic girdle actually no way. I'd never really have strangled Roy

Licorice laughed then inviting us all to join in. What is wrong with exaggerating, we all like a good story, and that's part of what this film is about we don't even know if anything we're trying to show is true. Nan has no history there's no birth or marriage or death records for her, she's just a name with a horrible legend attached. A bogeywoman. Was Nan a giant? Perhaps I should imagine I'm playing the attack of the fifty foot woman when I'm being her. Ha. Stomping like Godzilla in her nettle dress. I could rip the top off that bloody windmill then no need to pussy around sticking notes through the door. Licorice and Pete could string it with microphones to their heart's content, a network of wires on each floor to catch the differing sounds of the building as it responds to the day and the night and the rain, infinitesimal shifts going on in its materials because they're brand new even if they're modelled as closely as possible into the shape of the mill that burnt down over a hundred years ago. Fire always a hazard in mills because of heat generated by the friction of the stones and flour in the air can act like gunpowder, Licorice says

Rain like diamonds and arrows sunbeams strike the land with their incredible power. Sheep wandering fucking and breeding little half brothers and sisters

England's wealth is built on their wool plunge your
hands in among the grease when you see it caught on
fences and thorns it never looks like much punctured
clouds perchance you're never going to get her back
Roy if you stare that fucking obvious way. Not that
I care. Not that I fucking care. I'm on borrowed time
here as it is, heart a little bit in my mouth every
time the door goes or the phone rings. Which is silly
I know there are loads of people who've overstayed
longer than I have so why should they target me
but it isn't a situation where logic applies I've read
horror stories about the detention centres and
I wouldn't be eligible for asylum there's nothing I'm
escaping from I just don't want to go back. Because
here is my home now. I made a pact with myself that
I would stay to the end of August before booking
my flight, that everything would be alright up till
then, that we would finish the film and that's why
I got Pete on board. He's the only one who is aware of
my true situation. I had heard he had some funding
left over and he knew about my legendary script.
My script may be a legend but it is very real, I said,
and if you co-direct with me your name will be on
it too. You'll get fifty percent of the credit. I'd timed
our visit to the pub so any moment now a troop of
Morris men should appear. I was curious to see how
he would react. We were both drinking G&Ts so
he'd already bucked a couple of my preconceptions.
What made you choose this story to base your film
around Licorice? No one else has done it, it's local,
no special effects required and gives me the chance to
explore a lot of things I'm interested in. All British
horror is folk horror, remember that? I want to test

out how far that is true. He poured the last crumbs of a packet of cheese and onion crisps into his palm and tipped them down his throat. English horror, not British. Sorry? *English* horror roots itself in the land, celebrating its muck and grooving on the old ultraviolence. People cling dumbly to traditions because they are things they've always done not because there's anything good about them. No one makes any attempt to understand why they act the way they do. They look on anything new, anyone from outside, with fear and suspicion. Any 'different' element entering an English horror film has to be consumed before it can threaten their 'way of life'. With a subset where it's *necessary* to consume the stranger in order for that way of life to carry on. He coughed like a shard of crisp had got stuck in his throat then gave me a shrewd look. I smiled to acknowledge I was getting his drift. And Scottish horror is different how exactly Pete? It's not *all* that different. Maybe a wee bit more metaphysical. I see. Whereas all English horror is anti-metaphysical, he went on. There's no interest in finding out why things are the way they are, how humans think about their place in the universe. They basically just don't want to know about anything beyond their own precious sacred dirt. What about *Frankenstein*? Oh well you have me there Licorice. His mouth twitched up then he turned, I followed his nervous glance around the pub. Oh hark the sound of bells. And clackety sticks. You like this kind of thing? Who just inconspicuously swiped to video.... You consider yourself an anthropologist of the English, Licorice? Ha ha ha ha what option do I have

Hearts and flowers and other such sweet olde
English things. Pothooks weathervanes in whatever
shape you fancy rolling pins blown out of glass and
stoppered full of your lover's breath. Keep it safe and
your sailor boy will return again let it break and he'll
sink to Davy Jones's locker at the bottom of the deep
blue sea. Roy is wearing a bright red beanie white
T-shirt wonder how much it cost and combat pants he
really doesn't look the part. Angie sports a long floaty
skirt and black lace top my bestest hat has never
quite recovered from Roy's bum squashing it on our
last holiday in Spain. She's brought sandals to better
practice walking in bare feet. Herbs crushed between
her sparkling toes there's thyme and marjoram
some kind of mint blurring into deliciousness. She
stretches out on the turf and shuts her eyes. For a
miracle it is hot today the sun Pete and I have been
waiting for has banished every cloud from the sky.
When I sit down beside her, she smiles without
opening her eyes and reaches for my hand. I can
feel what you're thinking Licorice don't worry there
is nail varnish remover in Pete's boot. Roy turns
his head. He must be boiling in that hat pissed off
with me for banning him from having his usual
metrosexual trims. He looked to Pete when this first
came up but Pete is fed up with Roy still sleeping
on his floor. Breathing his air twenty-four seven a
six foot two, ripped, pumped reminder that Angie
is unlikely ever to fall for him. You could always just
shave your head, he suggested with an apparent
helpfulness that made Angie snort and Roy give a
bad-tempered shrug. That would work, wouldn't
it, Licorice? It would, I allowed, uncomfortable at

Pete's backhanded support sucking me into their emotional triangle, but be very very clear about this Roy it's not something that I'm asking you to do

Pete and I didn't always see eye to eye. Two days earlier during a production meeting in my kitchen we had argued about using the golden ratio to set up shots. It started calmly enough with my remarking the ratio was a much more interesting way to break down frames than the good old rule of thirds. Pete was in like Flynn turns out he is a Fibonacci nut and after ten minutes I was wishing I'd never mentioned it. For certain shots yes, I repeated, where we want a particular effect. When we first see Nan collecting wood and her hand is bleeding from the brambles so she wipes it on her coat you can go as Raphael on that as you like. Other shots we want a completely different mood remember that book of papercuts I showed you kind of creepy-cute intimate and clumsy that's what it should feel like when Nan and Thomas meet. It leads to a rape scene. We're not filming that rape. We have to show how Thomas gets so under Nan's skin she doesn't flee when she has the chance and we can't do that according to the golden ratio and if this scene fails nothing in the film will make any sense. According to the narrative you've constructed Licorice. Pete the time for you to question my narrative is long past. You say it'll look like a puppet show if I use a jumpy handheld camera but you know what that's actually my backup plan if Roy and Angie don't deliver the goods. You're dissing something you don't understand I'm not going to have it all looking like Tess of the fucking d'Urbervilles. Pete eyeballed me

hard a sudden terror but I had no intention of giving
any ground: if he shops me to immigration I will
destroy his reputation from wherever I end up. Pete
I am listening to you. We'll discuss what we want in
each scene work out a shooting schedule and divide it
between us. You'll probably be shooting the majority
I'm giving you a fucking huge carrot you twitchy bastard. I didn't say the last bit. Oh aye Licorice. What
could possibly go wrong

If we could work out exactly what we wanted to
get from the windmill, maybe we'd be able to achieve
it somewhere else. If it was entirely a question of
dimensions then we could just scale something
miniature and string it with the tiniest, cheapest
mikes scraped from old devices. Bruised and damaged with my fingerprints all over them they'd
produce an interesting kind of feedback hum. I would
put the finished structure on my windowsill for
the air to make patterns through its cracks and slits.
An Aeolian harp of sorts, Pete commented, very
cool. Right up there on the list of humanity's most
beautiful comparatively harmless inventions. I burst
out laughing when he propositioned me strange that
should actually clear the air between us. Us both
being unbeautiful as you so charmingly put it isn't
really a good enough reason for us to fuck and frankly
I'm surprised though not flattered you asked since
most guys assume I'm a lesbian though if they paid
any kind of attention they'd notice girls don't go for me
either. I haven't the time Pete and you already know
it. What the fuck would you have done if I had said
yes? Nothing ventured nothing gained honey. Fair

enough want to hear what I'd actually do if I had
any amount of time? Can't really say no can you after
that? Well I'd be back in those small electricals recycling bins and build a whole string of little harps
right here in my kitchen. Arrange them a stone's
throw apart on the Downs so everyone in the vicinity
could hear the beautiful sounds of the air rather
than the traffic. My turn to ask what you mean by
beautiful, Licorice. Of course I'm not wishing to
turn the clock back I have no desire to banish the
railway or dual carriageway and yes I'm very much
aware I wouldn't be here if planes didn't exist do
you think that doesn't cross my mind every time
I purge a vapour trail from a shot of the sky? It would
be a temporary, mediated intervention in nature. An
aural mapping of humanity's historical exploitation
of the area. Giving the land its voice back ha ha ha.
I can see what you're thinking Pete you can write it
up as a proposal if it's any use to you. Have it on me.
I'd rather you answer my question Licorice at least
tell me what you think the effect on the listeners
would be. Coming across it unprepared. The sounds
from no traceable source. The hills are alive. Don't
really want me to generalise do you Pete? It would
make them think wouldn't it? Licorice I'll tell you for
free it would scare me shitless

Remember our family outing to the old post mill yes
the one with tea and tremendous value home-made
cakes way back when Roy and Angela were still
an item? The old boy who guided us called the great
beam that trundles its track round the mill so the
sweeps can best harvest the wind the tailpole.

That carries the fantackle, a much smaller windmill looking far more like those ones you see for sale down by the beach and its sails are positioned in perpendicular alignment with the main sweeps geared to some complicated toothed mechanism I'm not going to pretend I understand. Once the prevailing wind is blowing directly on the fantackle it can no longer move and then the big sweeps are perfectly aligned to utilise the wind. Our mill hasn't got a fantackle yet so its sweeps can't turn automatically into the wind which suits my purpose for the moment: my interest is in exploring the void this building encloses because it's been rebuilt on the original footings so many times. Four pillars of brick support two mighty crossbeams and the post on which the mill turns rises from their intersection braced with huge struts that form the bones of the low roundhouse at the mill's base. Exposed to rain and sun and the rambling tread of man and beast for over a hundred years but an old postcard kept its memory alive. If I'd been here then I'd have stood in the centre of the old footings and visualised the huge post directly above me thicker than I could embrace holding the weight of the building and the millstones weighing tonnes as it trundled round. Angie has said it reminds her of Baba Yaga's house. Not that it has hen's legs and sure it can't move anywhere except around its post. It is made of wood. But it's not ramshackle. In fact maybe what I find so scary is that it's fucking pristine. A giant white shining tooth sticking up out of the landscape. You're not going to show it in the film? No no that would be a distraction

At first I couldn't recollect if she and Roy had climbed all the way up when we visited the old mill. Pete definitely had because I remember hanging back so he would ascend the ladder in front of me. Not that Pete would have been bothering to look at my skinny arse but all the same. I waited until he had pulled himself through the trap onto the next floor before I placed my foot on the first rung. He already had a laminated scale drawing in his hand and announced this is the bin floor. Yes those do look like the grain bins over there. Licorice, I find it a lot easier to get things straight in my head if I speak them out loud. Sorry you know and in a way you're lucky you wear glasses when you get a bit older like me you'll be able to push them down your nose to read small print I just can't see it. What's this 'gurt big thing' lying across the floor? The windshaft. Is that what conveys the power generated by the sweeps down to the floor below to turn the stones? Really wouldn't want to get my arm stuck in there some noise it must make when the mill is working. Like an avalanche or claps of thunder. Is that what it says on the card? They're not grinding today are they I mean there's no chance this is all going to suddenly start turning? No grain in this bin, Pete remarked from where he had climbed up on part of the mechanism, in a way that would have properly upset the nice old boy who guided us, to peer over its edge. Oh wait. He licked his palm and drew it out again studded with grains do you want some Licorice? Eeuggh no. Suit yourself they're quite tasty. I peered down through the trap for any sign of Angie and Roy did the others come up Pete can't say I noticed they've probably sloped off somewhere for a

quick canoodle. Good luck to them I'm sure they can
still absorb the atmosphere while having a romantic
time. 'Twas then I spotted Roy's red and green
checked shirt pressed up against some sacks Angie's
long golden hair spread over everything whispers
and moans and lips and hands moving at a rate of
knots. Because I was craning at such an odd angle
above the trap I felt suddenly unbalanced. When I
sat back on my heels and glanced over at Pete he was
waiting to meet my gaze. A faint smile. Conniving.
Curious. Both of us peeping toms. He would have
had a much better view of what they were doing
through that gap between two floorboards over by
the bins. Like I said, Licorice. Your lovers are doing
what they do best. So we're stuck here Pete. We're
not stuck Licorice unless you really have a problem
with disturbing them. The slightest squeak of either
of the ladders and they'll spring apart: be zipping
and buttoning and smoothing their hair by the time
we get down they'll have managed to wipe even the
sheepish grins off their faces. Well we haven't seen
everything on this floor yet. What's that big hook up
above the bins? That my dear Licorice is the sack
hoist. And behind the sweeps where this wind shaft
goes into? That's the brake wheel. Funny I never
actually thought about how they'd be stopping this
thing. But when there's no more grain they would
have had to before the stones ground themselves to
pieces emitting dangerous sparks.... I shrugged. He
shrugged. Annoying cunt. Or is the brake wheel to
do with how they stopped the mill moving round any
further once they'd got it into position hang on

It always rained particularly hard on days we'd planned to reccy. I'd wanted us to go up to where three old dew ponds clustered at a meeting of the ways on the top of the Downs to scout it as the location where Nan and Thomas would first meet. Only one of the ponds ever held any water and even when it was dry rushes or water weeds of some kind seemed able to wait out on its bottom so it was a much brighter green than the surrounding turf. The other two had been dry for how many centuries and were almost hidden by gorse prickly sweet yellow flowers when the gorse blooms it's kissing time well you know these days that means all year round. With the land rolling away as far as the eye can spy in all directions, these thickets provide a welcome if uncomfortable shelter for rabbits sheep dogs walkers caught short and guerilla film-makers. But why three ponds so close together? I thought it most likely they had existed in succession. Their construction on free-draining chalk was a tricky business necessitating the creation of a watertight liner its traditional material clay hauled up over the Downs by ox-cart: once the clay (mixed with straw) had been spread over the pond base, the oxen would be led into the middle then round and round in gradually increasing circles so their hooves trampled — in the local parlance 'stoached' — every little last bit of the clay down tight. Then you waited for the pond to fill up dew would make its rarefied contribution especially if a tree gathering condensation overhung the spot but the donkey work was done by rain and if there was a very dry spell the shallow water would evaporate and the clay could crack and start to leak

No chance of getting up there today the cloud is
so low it completely occludes the ridge. Absolutely
mental Pete said I mean how high is it? Less than
250 metres. Might as well get in a pint and a hot
meal probably it'll clear later on but if we try to climb
up there now we won't be in a state to make use of
it. The pub stood on the old street that formed the
heart of the village. Though only August someone
had taken the decision to light the fire which would
have been great except the weather or some unknown
obstruction in the chimney meant the huge old
fireplace wasn't venting as it should. Therefore the
lounge smelled of smoke. The few other peeps in on
a Tuesday lunchtime remained at the bar desultorily
chatting to the landlord but we decided we didn't
care, any kind of fire was welcome as we were feeling
chilled after just staring up at the path towards the
dew ponds and besides we wanted to order food.
We could stand a little kippering. A white girl with
braids — who must have been the daughter of the
house since she didn't look old enough to be working
there — darted in poked the fire savagely and stood
there irresolutely swinging the poker watching
the result of her labours with evident displeasure.
Then she grabbed a free local paper off one of the
vacant tables and spread it in front of the hearth.
Rummaging behind the bar she produced a block of
firelighter and with a little knife that must normally
have been used for slicing lemons and limes began
shaving the block onto the paper and every time
she'd got a small heap of paraffin curls she would
throw them onto the fire and for a second or two the
flames would whoosh bright yellow. I'm really not

meant to do this, she said without turning round.
But the wood burns much better this way. You'll have
a nice warm fire. You do whatever you need to darling
we won't tell, Pete replied. Just mind yourself we
don't want you going up in smoke you won't look so
cute without eyebrows. He tapped the side of his
head. Another drink chaps? Roy was closely studying
one of the beer mats is there a joke or a special
offer on there ha ha ha neither oh fuck he sneezed
suddenly then again Pete and Licorice blessed him
simultaneously jinks padlock I'm sticking to beer

Angie drained her second gin & juice then excused
herself to the ladies. Neither Roy nor Pete seemed to
notice that after twenty minutes she still hadn't
returned so no point alerting them: I got up from the
table and walked down the chilly passage towards the
smell of disinfectant not quite masking the smell of
piss. Basin. Mirror. Bin. Plastic flowers. Two cubicles
both apparently engaged. Angela? Are you okay in
there? It's Licorice, I added then thought what a fool
for who else was it going to be. I'm alright, Angie's
voice came very quietly from the cubicle on the right.
Don't worry Licorice. I'm fine. Good, I answered not
quite convinced. Is there anything you need? Glancing
round, the bathroom lacked one of those machines
dispensing overpriced sanitary protection and
condoms though there were two very deep rawl plug
holes high on the wall where it might once have been
attached. Do you have your period? I said in the quiet-
est clearest voice I could manage, conscious of the
occupant of the left hand cubicle if indeed there was
someone inside listening to everything we said.

I have tampons in my bag, I can get them if you need them. Ibuprofen too if you're in pain. No Licorice I'm okay. I haven't got my period

Silence then the sound of the snib being drawn back so the door eased open. Come in if you like. The cubicle had a tiny barred window out onto the garden. It was freezing. Angie was perched fully clothed on the toilet seat. Her eyes were swollen but she had evidently cried herself out. It's kind of you to be concerned about me Licorice. Or did you come in for a pee ha ha. Use this one if you like the other cubicle seems to be locked up. I'm okay thanks, I said then. I don't need to pee. Just as well since I seem to have used up all the bog paper. Have a tissue. Thanks. She took a while to wipe her nose. She'd have liked me to say Roy had asked me to check on her but she already accepted that wasn't the case. They're probably tucking into their food by now she pulled a face in the mirror and ran her fingers upwards through her hair. I'm not hungry. How about you Licorice? I shook my head though the thought of the fish chips and minted peas I'd ordered cost me quite a pang. I need some fresh air, Angie said. Have you got an umbrella in that bag? Licorice you are a regular Mary Poppins

Out in the garden even the seats beneath the sun-shades were wet. Angie crouched against one shivering but she refused to go back to the bar what with the smell of smoke and paraffin in that room I was feeling really sick. I'm much better out here. Why don't we go down the road? What bits of the village would have been here in Nan's time Licorice?

I was trying to hold the umbrella over us both which meant I had to lengthen my stride and dodge puddles and talk not the easiest of combinations. Defo the Norman church which looks pretty much the same as it did back then. The pub where we've left our friends guzzling is old enough too though it would have been a newish cottage in Nan's day with I don't know how many people living in it. And the windmill Licorice you and Pete seem so preoccupied by it. I allowed that I wasn't positive it would have existed at the precise spot. Definitely there would have been a post mill here in Nan's time. It would have been owned by the lord of the manor not that he'd have been doing the milling ha ha ha. Post mills are recorded in England from the twelfth century. Tower, smock and fan mills came later as people figured out ways to make just the very top of the windmill holding the sweeps as they call them round here move into the wind: these more robust structures were less likely to be toppled by a gale. Actually the posts of the very earliest mills were set directly into the ground but that meant the wood rotted and the whole thing could collapse without warning. Elevating the post on its beams and footings strikes me as a much better design it must have been a whole lot easier to turn a post that wasn't embedded in a shaft going down into the earth can we stop a moment here Angie I really need to get my breath. You're shivering now I'm being so selfish here give me the brolly Licorice I'll hold it over us both. Are you asthmatic? Take it easy love. Have you got an inhaler? No no just very occasionally I feel like I've forgotten how to breathe. I just have to clear my mind then I remember. Angie used her free hand to squeeze

mine. Your hands are even colder than mine oh well
you know what that's supposed to mean. A car raced
past honking rudely. Dip your lights bastard not our
fault there's no fucking pavement

Can we get to the mill this way? It's a few hundred
metres. I'll turn my phone torch on then these cars
will have even less excuse for running us down.
Country roads are always a nightmare round my
nan's too oh god you do know I'm talking about my
granny down in Devon right *not* Nan Kemp and
arrggh! I'm super sorry Licorice I swear your English
is better and more idiomatic than mine this is a huge
pile of shit I'm digging myself into. The crossroads
ahead is where she was hanged isn't it? I know the
windmill's thataway but can we just go up the other
road for a bit? So here's a VR postbox looking kind
of blobby under its century of red paint. Let's say
half a million letters — only a hundred a week for a
hundred years — have been pushed through its slot.
Business letters love letters dunning letters letters to
friends brief notes telling your parents how you are
getting along just dandy birthday cards bills circulars
Christmas cards postcards. At one time it would
have been stuffed full every day and now there's vir-
tually nothing *in* there. She rapped lightly with her
knuckles, turning away with a frown. What's on that
noticeboard over there Licorice? Bloody rain has
got in behind the perspex and made everything inkjet
run. Community policing by WPC Lisa? Laura?
Shame the photo's so faded probably she looks quite
cute in her little flat hat. Got her work cut out for
her round here can you imagine the gangs the drugs

the serious organised crime? Yet what do I know for starters that kid in the pub is obviously a pyro

The Women's Institute they've got to be kidding me does it still exist? Hey some of their guest speakers look quite interesting wonder if you get tea and cake or a free glass of ladypetrol thrown in? Licorice you and I should give a talk to them once the film is finished. They've filled their schedule up until Christmas but how about one week next spring? Look here's the email address we should send in a proposal all about your take on the legend of Nan Kemp. Couldn't be of more local interest this noticeboard is practically on top of where she was hanged. Are you thinking it's too grim for them? You've got so many interesting ideas about why the story developed the way it did and all that sociological stuff you come out with about how it reflects the position of women at the time. All those literary sources too remember when you were telling me about stories where children get eaten by giants and ogres crazy stuff. You think it's a good idea? You're actually up for it? Sure Angie if we do it together and you're prepared to talk about the experience of playing Nan: as long as you don't mind that you will inevitably be asked what it was like to get inside the skin of someone who killed her own kids and fed them to her husband. I'd probably say once you've killed your kids cooking them isn't such a stretch ha ha just joking. Seriously it's bloody difficult because I find that level of hatred hard to understand. I mean if Nan wasn't criminally insane, or evil, if she was actually functioning in any kind of mental space that centuries later I could even imagine touching, what terrible things must her husband have done to her to drive her to take such an extreme revenge. I've said I've hated people and sure I felt like killing Roy when I found out he'd fucked me over with Elaine. Briefly. But that feeling has totally settled into schadenfreude I actually enjoy feeling a tiny bit sorry for him now watching Pete trample on his toes and even you Licorice bully him a little. Not that I'm saying he doesn't deserve it. And Licorice I can tell what you're thinking it's easier for me when I see him being so miserable. And homeless. If he'd shacked up with bloody Elaine if everything in the garden was rosy for him it would have been much harder for me to deal

But you know Licorice I'm really relieved I don't still hate him. Because if I felt such a very strong emotion it might be the tails side of love and flip back again if I was stupid enough to let it. I'm just okay without Roy now we had some very good times together but I've moved on. Not that I'm looking for anyone else in a hurry I don't need another relationship and that feels good too. When I look in the mirror I'm definitely not unhappy. I've got so much more time than I've had for ages: I'm reading books I always meant to watching the box sets *I* want to watch without considering what Roy can stand. I've even put an app on my phone to relearn the French I took at school. Sometimes I feel England is fucking finished if I can get my French up to scratch I'm going to move to Paris next year. Roy and I had a romantic weekend there on Airbnb but sightseeing wasn't high on our agenda we just got out of bed to eat and drink.

Sorry have I shocked you Licorice mind you that
was good he's always been picky about where he eats
you know reads all the reviews and likes to try those
quirky specialities he wouldn't get anywhere else.
No grabbing a quick burger and fries when you're out
with Roy. He's even a good cook when he makes the
effort. Ha. Could have been a lot more often. Anyway
the view from our room was literally the legs of the
Eiffel Tower straddling a whole load of roofs. I mean
you see postcards of the tower and it's in the middle of
an empty space but from our vantage point it looked
like there were buildings underneath. We couldn't see
beyond the base of the main shaft but these fucking
massive open ironwork legs dwarfed even the highest
of the higgledy-piggledy roofs with their chimneys
aerials receiving dishes fire escapes and other bits
and bobs sticking up. By the end of the weekend
I felt I'd done the Eiffel Tower even though I never
paid my money to set foot on it. You've never been to
Paris? If I get myself a place you've absolutely got to
come and stay. We can flaneuse the streets together
maybe you'll come up with the idea for your next film.
The most important thing you've taught me Licorice
is how when your surroundings are brand new and
strange you should treat everything as a gift rather
than a threat. How long does that last? Do you get
used to it? How do you feel about that now Licorice

Roy has developed a cough that keeps me awake
at night I say it's some weird reverse psychosomatic
side-effect of swapping fags for a patch ha ha but
Roy blames me and Licorice for keeping him out in
all weathers. Off to the gym at the crack of dawn

every morning after shovelling down his power fuel.
He can't really think he'll get Ange back by acquiring
bigger muscles: perhaps he's fantasising about
ripping off the head of anyone lucky enough to replace
him but I don't see it myself he's not a violent guy. I've
bought an airbed to stop him moaning about my sofa
so now he moans he has to pump that up every night.
Faulty return valve bruv. So I'm a cheapskate. So it's
a bit more exercise for you what's the problem when
you love exercise so much you miserable cunt? Never
tell Licorice how I dreamed about Ange last night.
Waking in a muck sweat even though I was sleeping
in the buff. Embarrassing. Sheets soaked. No chance
of going back to sleep. At least as Roy wasn't there I
could go through and switch on my big screen. Close
the curtains. Think of Licorice in her kitchen two
floors below. I could text and see if she wants to come
up and view the footage with me. But why should I
wake her up if she's actually managing to sleep?
To make myself feel less of a sad sick boy because I
wouldn't then be watching that footage of Angela
screaming and spinning round in her rain-soaked
dress all by myself? Over and over on repeat with the
sound turned off so I'm just zooming in on her face.
Eyes closed most of the time so when she blinks the
water away from her lashes it's shall we just draw
a veil over that and watch her do it again. A sound
outside like a bell struck very clearly. It's much
later than one o'clock. Carried over from the train
station? There it goes again. Someone's phone alarm.
Thank christ they've woken up. Is it Licorice? Well
she's not texting me. No Pete you big slob get your
arse down here I've done another hundred sketches

showing exactly what I want your shots to capture just to rub in that I've given you an impossible task.... Whatever, Licorice. Kind of a shame she never put her Aeolian harp out on the kitchen sill. Kind of my fault. She told me she had second thoughts it would have driven the neighbours mad and I don't want to draw any more attention to myself. Maybe I'll ask her to give it to me when she leaves

Last night was the first time in ages I had my place to myself for Roy announced he was going to camp out up by the ponds. Under the stars. He, like me, had obviously studied the forecast and noted the zero chance of rain so I wasn't that impressed nor did I make any attempt to dissuade him. You've got all your stuff for tomorrow? Your iron rations? Charged your phone? Yes dad. Good luck practising your wilderness survival skills two miles from a fucking town was what I didn't say. Not that he'll be needing his iron rations in fact I bet he'll have popped down to that pub for a hearty supper. Putting away a huge dish of rabbit pie with ale gravy or a local lamb shank so tenderly slow-cooked its meat just kind of floats apart in your mouth could count as honing his craft from one angle I suppose and if you're going to be lying on the ground in a one season sleeping bag letting your phone teach you late August's constellations a full belly's definitely a good idea. Washed down with a few pints no doubt not that Roy's a big drinker. But sitting there on your own to wait out closing time what else you going to do? And that mad kid? Christ. I'd almost forgotten her. She's way too young to be serving in the bar but mummy

and daddy might have her washing up in the kitchen
what's wrong with earning your pocket money young
lady the sooner you're back at school the. Or she
might have sashayed through the bar on her way
back in from Guides or. Jesus. What is fucking wrong
with me. I mean Angela...shit. Think it through
then Pete if you put it to the back of your mind it'll
never leave you alone. Make it like a scene in the
film. What's her name going to be? Chloe? How about
Jeanette...or Savannah. Last time I went to London
whiny kid opposite watching jingly pink crap on
mum's iPad was Savannah. If this one glimpses Roy
through the swing doors from the kitchen she's going
to remember him for sure. Suppose she ignores all
her instructions and brings his rabbit pie out with
her own hands. Careful this plate is *very* hot. Here's
your cutlery. Can I get you any condiments? You
was in the other day wasn't you with your friends.
Your girls disappeared so it was just you and the
Scottish guy and you had an argument about who
was going to pay for the fish and chips the Chinese
lady ordered. What's your name mate? My name
is Tom, Roy might say then to try it out. Savannah
shrugs. I've got two Toms already in my class actually
one calls himself Tommie and the other's a right
little dirtbag. No offence, Tom. None taken. How's
the pie? It's very good amazing hint of wild thyme...
or is it marjoram? Pastry light as a feather. And the
meat is so flavoursome wow are the rabbits caught
around here? You'd have to ask my mum Tom I don't
take any interest in that sort of thing. I'll pass on
your compliments to the chef. You a student at the uni
then you look like you could be. I was until recently.

Now I'm looking for a job. Not many of those going round here but I could put a word in with my dad for you if you like. Yeah thanks so nice of you to offer but tonight's actually my night off. I'm training to be a personal trainer. In a gym. Wow. You must be really fit and strong. Got to be so healthy all the time I never normally drink or eat pies and tonight I thought why don't I just enjoy myself for once and have a really good meal then I can walk it off on the way home. So I'm savouring each delicious mouthful. Where do you live then Tom must be quite some distance ha ha ha ha? Near the ferry terminal just off the access road for the industrial estate. Change of scenery for you round here then. You're not wrong. It's beautiful. It's alright I suppose is that why you came back

I'm inching my overfilled car its suspension already fucked up the narrow lane. Licorice hops out to open and close the gates. She jumps back in blethering no point putting my seat belt on again since it's not a public highway and Angela giggles because she doesn't understand how Licorice thinks about the cops. The grey-white garment Licorice has put her in looks ugly even on her she pokes out her tongue as I catch her eyes in the rear-view mirror do you have to joggle the car around so much Pete it feels like the cross Channel ferry in a heavy swell I'm so sorry about that my lady you can walk if you like and lighten the load. She opens the door before I stop course I'm alright in bare feet least I know now why Roy didn't want a lift. Roy used to call your car Christine Pete did you know that? Naturally Angela since I told him that was its name. I haven't told her he's been camping out up at the ponds. Round-headed rampion chalk milkwort and bastard toadflax quaking grass sheep's fescue burnt orchid autumn lady's tresses

Eyebright pasque flower sainfoin spotted cat's-ear lady's fingers centaury horseshoe vetch kidney vetch purple milk-vetch cowslip bird's foot trefoil (call it eggs-and-bacon if you want to feel peckish) devil's-bit scabious field scabious small scabious common knapweed fly orchid bee orchid fragrant orchid man orchid twayblade pyramidal orchid. Creeping thistle. Wild licorice or liquorice milk-vetch sometimes used for tea. Hawkbit lady's bedstraw agrimony mugwort I'm never going to walk over all those and if I did I wouldn't recognise them. Wouldn't expect you to only a few are in flower now. These are plants from all over the area you wouldn't be seeing every one round here though in theory they might grow if conditions were perfect there could be ancient but still viable seeds in the scratch soil atop of the chalk and with the orchids who knows about all that mysterious fungal-dependent underground network thing they have going on. Let's not forget the fungi scarlet waxcap slimy waxcap spangle waxcap smoky spindles puffball and earth star. With it having been so wet can we expect kilograms of mushrooms to have sprung up everywhere? Yum fried in garlic butter you know some of them fucking fairy rings are hundreds of years old moving outwards over time as their mycelia seek out fresh supplies of nitrogen in the soil. Any we see today Nan might have passed when they were much smaller. Maybe we should be sending you up the hill with a wee basket over your arm failing that a plastic bag. How about it Ange? Don't think *you* should be trusting me to work out which ones aren't poisonous or casting me as little red riding hood already ha ha ha. Even seven hundred years ago Licorice there wouldn't have been any actual wolves round here? No no no long since exterminated you know criminals under sentence of death could avoid execution as long as they brought in a stipulated number of wolf tongues every year. Set a beast to catch a beast. Not that Nan ever had her day in court. And that was how things had worked maybe a couple of hundred years before her time

Anyway I'm already carrying this phone you've given me Licorice so what did you want me to do again exactly? Just have the video on and film anything that strikes you as interesting. Don't worry about it Angie we are leaving it entirely up to you if you feel you can hack it great but by not doing it you're also expressing something. And if you notice modern discrepancies such as plastic bottle caps gum wrappers that bloody ubiquitous bright blue baler twine I don't want you to censor yourself. We can edit out afterwards anything that we feel doesn't fit. I just wanted to give you some kind of agency on your long climb up the hill. Think of the camera as your curious eyes. If the sound's on that's going to be footsteps and my increasingly laboured breathing unless I feel like talking to myself ha ha ha ha. You talk to yourself if you want or sing whatever comes into your head if you have enough breath, anything you feel like doing at all is good just let yourself go.

We've already done the set-up for this scene Angie I'm not going to direct you any more. Photograph whatever you want when you turn your head photograph the ground if you feel nervous about snakes they'll probably be frightened away by the vibration of your footfall in any case though I guess your bare feet won't have the impact of big clumpy boots. Up into the dazzling eye of the sun though don't you go damaging your eyes now. Forecast is twenty-seven later on are you wearing sunscreen? Actually no because when I start to sweat it's going to look all soapy. I've got this gorgeous unperfumed mineral stuff I can dust you with. No thanks Licorice I've been really fucking careful this morning didn't use soap or shampoo in the shower my hair's sticking up naturally from where I rinsed it left my anti-perspirant deodorant off too my pits are damp to prove it mmm the authentic smell and feel of womanly sweat! Don't tell Pete I'm not wearing a bra or any knickers it's so thick and heavy this fake homespun you've dressed me in. Had to sew three layers of fabric together to get the heft. Handstitched the top one look though the rest of it was run up on the machine. Really tried to get that sag and wrinkle on the seam like it's never been pressed and all the many times it's been wet means the fabric finally smells right. You're a very talented seamstress Licorice. Give you lessons if you like Ange it'd be a whole new string to your bow

Still what counts is how do you feel wearing it? Tell you the truth Licorice I feel bloody strange. I can almost imagine this dress *is* made of nettles and you know what I did a bit of research and found out that

nettles are meant to be proof against enchantment.
Which must be because their painful sting brings you
back to reality puncturing whatever illusion you've
been caught in. Same deal with holly. Thistles?
Gorse? No idea but please remember to be careful of
thistles where you're walking. Nan would have been
careful too even if her soles were as tough as ha ha ha
old boots. The other weird thing Licorice is that
I'm already so hungry. Did you have breakfast sure
a couple of chunks of that stoneground bread you
bought. Couldn't put margarine or marmite or
marmalade on it. Honey I could have had if there was
any in the cupboard but it would have been the cheap
stuff blended out of pollen gathered from flowers
all over the world: much too global for our Nan mind
you I guess even local honey would contain nectar
from lots of kinds of plants that didn't grow here
when she was alive. Oilseed rape in spring that mad
bright yellow smelling faintly of mustard. Exactly.
I drank half a pint of milk though I was thinking
all the time it wouldn't have been anything like the
milk Nan would have drunk. All the lovely dangerous
microbes not stripped out of it for a start and not
homogenised either or cold from being in my fridge.
I never normally drink milk and I can feel it sloshing
in my stomach right now. Or could be butterflies I
suppose. Of course I wasn't making tea or coffee this
morning: no minty fresh toothpaste for me so can't
be distracting myself from thinking I'm a fourteenth
century wench by my own coffee breath

There is a huge slippage between how the landscape
would have looked back then and how it is now we

just have to hope people will get so caught up in the
story they won't care. If we'd wanted something
that looked obviously authentic we could have shot
at the hillfort, carefully avoiding the signs, but
then why would a fourteenth century girl go up to
the hillfort, it would have been abandoned so many
generations back and everything of use removed.
What reason would Nan have to be curious about
that past? You've done great preparation Angie and
now you need to put all of it away at the back of your
mind. You've considered the things Nan wouldn't
have been familiar with and would therefore have
noticed as anomalies. Now you have to forget about
anything which might distract you from thinking
you're a girl who lived seven hundred years ago. You
have to forget that your mouth feels fuzzy. You have
to forget about what you didn't have for breakfast.
You have to forget that you're sweating and your
armpits stink and when you feel the sun tickle your
skin don't think about sunburn or cancer risk.
No hole in the ozone layer in Nan's time ha ha ha.
Of course it's impossible to know what *her* weather
would have been like. It might just about have been
the mini Ice Age after the medieval warm period
please don't think about mammoths and glaciers
because it was nothing like that. Colder and wetter
than today though would have made farming harder
less money and less food though we don't know Nan's
background we can assume this was something
she suffered from? Our story is set before the Black
Death since you ask Angela one theory about the
'little ice age' was its cold wet weather suppressing
crop yields year on year produced a hungry population

in poorer health with zero resistance to disease however another expert has fingered the Black Death's spectacular mortality as root cause of this global cooling since much of the land under cultivation all across Europe was abandoned and its subsequent re-wooding meant the trees acted as a carbon sink. You can pick whichever floats your boat but trying to film a rewilded landscape would have been so much harder for us today

So yes Angie walking up the hill in our beautiful brilliant sunlight today you'll probably be warmer than Nancy would ever have been. You can use this though can't you, if you imagine living somewhere without electric light or heating, not even glass in the windows, damp and black and mouldy yeah it does sound a bit like our second floor shower room Pete. How good it would have been to lie in the sun feeling it all over your skin thinking about it baking through to your bones. Finally the snotty nose that has persisted through a wet June July and almost all of August has dried up. So when you're walking up the hill in the sunlight you're not caring about the ruined crops down below. The barley the wheat little bit of flax your dress is made from peas and beans and onions rotting on the stalk. The bees and butterflies are out in force today because it's sunny and there's not a whisker of a breeze. Small tortoiseshell meadow brown gatekeeper orange tip brimstone green hairstreak wall comma common blue adonis blue chalkhill blue small blue ringlet dingy skipper small skipper grizzled skipper marbled white my favourite one of all painted ladies migrating in huge

clouds peacock red admiral and very exceptionally
the duke of burgundy might dart up from just in
front of your feet. Sure it's the vibration of your tread
that startles them up but also their ceaseless quest
for food coupled with peripatetic skirmishing over
territory and mates. Grazing on dung and tufts of old
sheep's wool to supply the salts nectar lacks. Those
little odd humps are anthills where red and black
ants have been taking care of adonis blue larvae
burying them at night away from predators in order
to milk the sweet juice from their honey glands

So where the fuck is Roy, Licorice? I had asked
when I was standing there with Pete watching her
get her stuff together only to have her tell me that
he's been up by the bloody ponds all night. WTF?
Roy? Camping out? Not his style at all. I don't know
Licorice shrugged maybe he wanted a change from
Pete's floor. She didn't make eye contact with me
then was she being disingenuous or wanting to dis-
courage me from thinking along those lines. She had
just taken all her gear out of her rucksack and was
painstakingly counting it back in again. Nerves.
Her little ritual. A fucking thermos. Standing next
to me Pete had just the one camera in his hand. He'd
already tested the light of course it was changing
all the time but we're on the western side of the hill
here. Chasing dawn shadows. Licorice's laughter
then sounded weak and cracked in the still air.
Dawn Shadows, she repeated. What a name that
would be. She clipped her rucksack shut and slung it
over her shoulders, trapping her ponytail under
one of the straps then yanking it free. Okay I'm off.

I'll text you once I'm in position. Here's to this not turning out a hot mess. We watched her climb the path. Slight figure in black, black rucksack, baseball cap, big grippy boots so she was going much faster than I would. Already a black ant crawling up the white chalk. Pete had raised his camera to follow her progress but it wasn't live. What the fuck did she mean by 'hot mess'? That was for me Ange it's what I said about the way she wants me to shoot. Nothing to do with you. See where she is now? He lowered the camera. When you reach that point on the path that's where I'll stop filming you

Scratch twitch hiss. He loves me not. Pull off the petals one after another then suffer a change of heart I have daisy chains on my wrists and around my neck I like your take on things Licorice I like your style. She came into the shop where I was working a few times not sure if she remembers but no way am I bringing it up. She'd often be sitting in the library not the study section upstairs but the bit with papers and mags at the front. She liked to get one of the window seats there and she'd either be craning over some publication drawing very intently in one of her small square sketchbooks or just gazing out into the square with her arms folded and a faint smile on her face looking a thousand miles away but actually absorbing like a fucking sponge whatever was happening right in front of her. I would have liked to speak to her. I'd seen a short she'd made years ago starring herself. Not on YouTube or Vimeo this was part of a reel of old student films someone put together for a festival and it was the one that stayed with me. Oh wow she clapped her hands when I finally told her it's years since I saw *that*. Does it look okay? I'm so glad you liked it. I was not my first choice to act but at least I didn't have to feel guilty about not paying me. This is marbling, the young fresh-faced spiky-haired Licorice intones in an accent much heavier than she speaks in today, like you see on the endpapers of old books, where you squirt drops of ink onto a tray of water and swirl it into elaborate patterns with a comb. Then you lay a sheet carefully on top and removing it just as carefully a perfect image of the pattern is transferred. Hey presto! In Licorice's hands this was not what happened. The patterns that emerged as the sheets were pulled off the water were not at all what was there in the ink. At first this was played for comedy with Licorice really hamming up her voiceover but as the film progressed (it was only ten minutes long) the sheets she pulled from the water bore increasingly disturbing images and her voiceover became ever more manic. It ended up with her pegging all the sheets of paper onto a liftomatic rotary washing line so the wind could spin them while she capered around it. *Whirligig* it was called so much more fucking compelling to watch than to describe and part of that was Licorice herself her performance the total crazy punk aesthetic she was into then. Fifteen years ago? How old is she now thirty-five forty

Shall we talk this scene through, Nan's motivation and Thomas's motivation. How do you see Thomas? Well now. One way of spinning the story is that he is literally a beast in human form. He seduces the innocent young Nan with his handsome face and fine words, enticing her to sit down on the grass beside him. He kisses her which she doesn't entirely resist and then brutally pushes her to the ground and rapes her. When she struggles and screams he forces his hand into her mouth to silence her. Or to cut off her breathing. She bites him. Ouch. We're not shooting any of that, Licorice declared. This is what happens after the scene we shoot. How are you conveying it then? Voiceover? Intertitular cards? Licorice sighed. I'll figure that out once we've shot *this* scene. There's all sorts of things we could do. Drawings. Either in my style or the style of the Luttrell Psalter. I *have* showed you. Don't you remember the picture of the blue post mill? Puppets, Pete said then. Couldn't quite resist a smirk. No no not puppets I've given up on that idea

Two empty chairs maybe? Back to back. Have to be the right kind of chairs not necessarily medieval but oak with a nicely worn patina and rush seats. Rush light on the floor maybe. Stink of tallow. A damaged interior there'd have been oxen living there as well? Even-toed ungulates remember the tiny cast shoe I showed you they'd have needed two on each foot and what a palaver shoeing would have been the ox was thrown to the ground and all four feet lashed to a heavy wooden tripod until the process was complete. Trundle the chairs around to face each other for another court scene that never happens: Thomas's trial for rape. Rape was one of only two crimes for which a woman could bring a prosecution under English law at the time, Licorice

said, the other being if her husband was actually killed in her arms, but how likely was it that Nan would
successfully prosecute Thomas? She might have
pleaded the loss of her virginity if she was able to
present the court with evidence of torn clothing and
her blood. If Thomas had been found guilty of raping
Nan he would have been castrated and his eyes put
out. However without forensics and DNA matching
Licorice sighed it really bothers me that this bothers
me how would the judges know the blood was Nan's?
Would they be prepared to trust her word and the
evidence of their own eyes? Had they some horrible
idea they could recognise the blood of the ruptured
hymen by its odour colour or sympathetic magic?
Convictions for rape in this historical period, Licorice
pointed out, were exceedingly rare. By this time Nan's
parents had realised she was pregnant and therefore
they accepted Thomas's offer of marriage. Nan's
agency was totally erased and the crime against her
effectively undone. Stuck with her handsome brutal
husband who now completely owned her body,
she was forced to endure his caresses, repeated
pregnancies and after delivery his babes snapping
like young crocodiles at her tits. Healthy vigorous
children seemingly immune from the diseases that
did for other people's kids: Thomas's handsome face
grinning back at her from all of them. Completely
dehumanised by the way she had been treated, the
only way Nan could register her protest (and find a
way out) was to execute such a grievous act on the
person she held responsible for her plight. The worm
turning. The biter bit. Nan numbly justified to herself even if everyone else considered her an evil,

unnatural monster. End of that particular story. But there were other ways to play it

As Nan I don't know any of this. Fucking concentrate Angie: I don't know Licorice or Pete or Roy I have never met Thomas before and have no idea he is going to be up at the fucking pond. Nan walks up to the pond just to see what was going on, or she might have been getting away from her mother and the endless tedious fucking chores. The roads have been there forever. Licorice told me about the small hoard of Roman coins had it fallen out of someone's pack or was it deliberately buried as some kind of insurance policy against an unknown future that was never cashed in. Fancy if Nan had found it! That would have been so cool. Farmers driving carts pulled by oxen I want you to imagine small thickset red shiny beasts, Licorice said: shepherds pasturing their flock on the sweet upland grass for the day, fetching them down in the evening to be corralled on a fallow field and enrich the poor soil with their dung for next year's crops. Fishwives with donkeys carrying their fish to market all the way from the sea only six or seven miles to the south extending its maritime influence the way she says that always makes me smile over the chalk. Have I ever even been that far? The path is mostly smooth going with grand vistas all around but this sharp descent down the northwest face of the hill is tricky and if the old biddies catch me hanging around they might call on me to help the donkeys with their heavy slippery baskets down the slope. Slap round the head. Eeuggh hate fish glazed eyes stinking on the chalk can't eat them raw. Hiding in the bushes until something more interesting comes along. Ground-nesting skylarks spiral up and away to distract potential predators but a girl like me who has grown up on the hill might have a handle on their manoeuvres and be able to spot, as I ramble, the nests with their tiny brown marbled eggs. If I find any will I be eating them raw there and then lightly cracking the shells to pour their contents down my throat: one brief swallow of yolk and albumen even the forming bird with its delicate bones I might draw the line at that but in any case the nest is ruined

Let's stick with Angela's point of view this cairn made of little bits of chalk marks the moment Pete stops filming me and texts Licorice to tell her I'm on my way. Two minutes, four minutes max is what they reckon. I said give me five in this blind spot in case Nan decides to sit down and do something. Licorice nods. Pete has now to wait three minutes before starting up the hill. He'll be there for whatever the end of this scene turns out to be. Licorice you just sitting in the bushes up there with your thermos waiting for me? Tea or coffee in there girl? Little steel cup warming your chilly hands. I am freezing. Not just that this fucking dress is making me sweat but the dew on the grass we're in shadow here means it's cold and damp and squidgy between my toes. Harder to grip. Put my arms out to balance. Take a selfie. Angela to camera: in the opening soliloquy she declares her true intent. Nice. Pull a face. Standing on one leg my bruised toes a crumpled magenta plastic bag are your trousers getting damp Licorice because it's not there for you to sit on? Careless lady or did you drop it a-purpose what about my ex-lover kipping up here last night? You hadn't got no tent or sleeping mat or groundsheet (said Pete). When you woke up this morning in your barely water-resistant sleeping bag was your face all covered with dewdrops condensing on your warm skin seeping through your subcutaneous fat and muscles to penetrate the marrow of your bones. Shepherd boy lazing on the hill that's what she decided to make you. Fucking stay in character. Put your drink down Licorice and pick up your camera when you think I'm going to come. You've got to have your eyes trained on the spot where I'm going to emerge. There on the path. Where we've rehearsed it. Where you've reccied the route. Made such a big deal of walking it yourself in bare feet. So to be sure there's nothing that can harm you Nan or Angela. All the timing, all the angles, adjustments of the light. Baseball cap pulled down on your forehead so the morning sun doesn't get into your eyes

What if I decide to surprise you. Go off the path. Climb up and come down with the sun at my back of course there's the little problem of the barbed wire fence but expect I can squeeze through it without too much damage thanks to your three layers of fabric. Here I am Licorice. Peekaboo. Now catch me girl. Sweet Angela, there is nothing here but us birds. Licorice has curled up and gone to sleep even the coffee couldn't keep her awake or maybe someone mickey finned it a couple of swigs and the cup fell from her nerveless hands she is snoring gently under the gorse bush among the prickles and golden flowers. She'll be fine when she wakes neck a little stiff from the odd angle but won't remember any of us it'll be like the past three months have completely blanked themselves. Pete will be the guy who's just moved in upstairs from you and Roy and Angela won't even be names on your radar. What the fuck am I doing here three dozen of your very best my good man sharp lines of twigs and wire dividing space did you hear the one about the guy who pissed onto an electric fence ha ha he won't be doing that again in no hurry. First two toenails on my right foot blackening hope it's a bruise not a fungal infection there is hardly any breeze even up here but I can't see the mill yet can I? Looks like the drawings Licorice posted through the door

Fuck yes. Intricate details of the film's scenes lie on the doormat in a massive heap mixed in with their regular post pizza leaflets cards to clean your gutters reiki empowerment are you serious Pete do you really think someone bunging flyers is going to trudge all the way up there depends on their manager Licorice some cunts'll follow you round in their car and intercept you to fucking check there's no sticker on the door indicating the residents don't want that kind of bumph. Not forgetting Pete's letters on the headed notepaper of his production company making everything seem as official as possible even a VAT number which worried me when I first noticed because have you just faked it when do you ever pay VAT. When he assured me that it was real and above board, that he had registered for VAT it freaked me out even more. I don't know why you're so concerned about it Licorice. Your name doesn't appear on any of the paperwork. We discussed that remember and you said that was how you wanted it. Any road I do all the paperwork properly, he added, submit my returns every three months even if there's nothing on them. The Revenue don't care. Why would you even bother when you don't have to? If I buy new equipment Licorice I can claim back the VAT twenty per cent on a few hundred quid is worth filling out a few forms for. Even stuff like stationery you know printing flyers too if we're going to publicise the film. Any extra processing we can't do between us. Website fees. Venue hire if we're wanting to show it somewhere like in the village hall you were saying about

Because you know Licorice it's not just about you getting to make your fucking masterpiece and then disappearing off. This film's not going in the back of a drawer even if that's what you'd want to happen. You don't really care? You lose interest once something is finished? Nice if you can afford to do that. Alright Pete call me out am I just plain lazy then. You know that's not my intention Licorice but since you've got me and Roy and Angela involved you surely see we need something out of this project for all our hard graft and energy and the time off work we've had to take. I mean Roy's got the fallback at the moment of being a fucking model or whatever it is he occasionally gets silly money for but he knows that's not going to be the case for ever there are younger cuter kids coming up and already the look is changing. And he's a good actor, I know I keep telling you that but I've worked with him before and he delivers, usually just at the point when you really

think he hasn't got it. That was the main reason
I suggested him because it seemed to be the kind of
brinkmanship you want. And what about our leading lady don't you care she'll be going back on the
tills directly we're finished up: she must have
taken all her annual leave to do this she needs it
to be something the right kind of people who could
give her work in the future will be able to see. And
yeah obviously I'm not thinking it's going to be any
kind of big commercial hit but with the right kind
of management it'll get round quite a few festivals.
Might pull in a prize or two you know with something
so quirky it's going to qualify for loads of categories.
I know how to be a pushy bastard. Come on Licorice,
don't pull a face, you know that was one of the
reasons you approached me

Only one cupboard in Licorice's kitchen has food in
it. Packets of cereal sachets of cup-a-soup packets of
instant noodles tubes of biscuits. Tins. You're forgetting the fridge! I've got all those fresh vegetables
in the fridge my diet is really extra healthy since I eat
them raw. You've got old film in the fridge too when
is that from and what are you keeping it for? Would
you throw it away Pete? Can't get it again for love nor
money. You can have it if you've got a use for it. She
smiles then irrefutably shutting me up because she
knows I don't. Have a biscuit Pete these ones are good
for dunking. Oh look couscous too that's not junk
food! Decided years ago not to buy anything I couldn't
prepare with hot water from the kettle so I could
get Mitzi to take out the cooker make space for my
workbench soldering irons blowtorch and suchlike.

Mitzi was a retired actress opera singer refugee from swinging London who'd washed up down here perhaps married into money anyway she was somewhere in her eighties and not fit enough to come over to the house any more. I paid my rent into her bank account every month that was as much contact as I'd ever had with her. But Licorice had been there so long when she moved in Mitzi was probably still a spry late middle-aged woman. Presumably at some stage in the last fifteen or twenty years Mitzi had said well how about it girl you're good at fixing things you keep an eye on the place for me and I won't ever put up your rent. The afternoon I moved in, Licorice was cleaning the stairs. My first glimpse of her was as a figure in a black baseball cap tightly shrouded in a black pinny: her clothes underneath were I never saw her in any other colour black as well. I had the feeling that she was purposefully cleaning the stairs when she knew I was arriving to get a good look at the new person in the house. The guy I'd rented the van from was on his way to another job and told me he hadn't contracted to carry all my shit up three steep flights. So he was throwing my boxes into the hall to get them out of his van as fast as he could and when he'd gone Licorice who had been apparently ignoring us up until then looked up from her regular swishing wringing lemony-scented motion with the mop and bucket and asked if I needed any help taking them up to the flat. Did she even ask? I can't remember. Maybe I had started up the stairs with a box in my arms and when I arrived at the flat door and set it down Licorice was behind me with another one. I can't get on with cleaning the hall until they're moved was what she said when I demurred. So that was how she knew I was a filmmaker. Or perhaps she knew anyway. I invited her in for a cup of tea to thank her but she said she had to get on. Another time perhaps. Smile. Basic relations established. If there's anything you need. Any problems in the flat. Come and ask me. Last door on the right on the first floor. I'm Licorice

Boxes of findings. Bags of material. Sewing machine. Yes you're right those are Roy's bodybuilding magazines out of the recycling. I keep them for papier-mâché. Unused sheets of gold silver and copper leaf and a tiny container full of salvaged scraps. Tubes of paint from the new to the nearly used up in what looked like the dish drainer, covered with dust. Once she noticed me looking at these and as a way of answering the question she imagined in my head fetched what she referred to as her log book: an oversized volume with crackling pages which contained photographs and watercolours, tipped in facing each other, of every object she had ever made. How did you get into this? She flipped back to the first double spread. Hmmm my space orientalist line this is — in questionable taste. I had made a short film using Kabuki-inspired masks which puzzled a lot of people because they didn't understand what use I was making of what they assumed was my heritage. Ha. Anyhow someone involved with this film must have seen it and figured to get me to make masks for them would be cheaper than someone who was established doing it for a living. The photograph showed the finished article whereas the watercolour had elements of a cutaway drawing, detailing the different layers. Notes in Licorice's small spidery writing about the materials used, where she'd sourced them and how the mask was supposed to work. I squinted at the page. Silvery net peels off, I read out. She shrugged. That's right. It did. Why? Oh Pete this is fifteen years ago I can't remember. I never saw the film so I don't even know if they used my masks in the end

What about *your* film Licorice? It was a comedy. I'd love to see it. She smiled and flipped forward through the book. Anyway that company employed me again so they obviously thought I did okay. Got into doing a lot of period stuff which I preferred because I didn't have to make it up out of my own head I could just study things and deconstruct them. Trips to the V&A to look at items from their special collections I always enjoyed getting to look at something that was usually kept in climate-controlled conditions and I had to handle wearing white cotton gloves, she laughed, to prevent my greasy twenty-first century fingerprints from shortening its life. I would take as many photographs from all angles, film it too, measure everything even the length of the stitches and when I came to make up the replica I would try to sew at least some of it the same way. My clients always got excellent value out of me because I would really go that extra mile to put something special into it. Still I made a good living as a freelance prop maker. Why did you stop Licorice? There was a time about five six years ago when it seemed like everyone had to tighten up their paperwork. So whenever I

submitted an invoice I would be required to put
my National Insurance number, my Unique Taxpayer
Reference on it. People never used to bother before.
And of course I had a UTR but I was. So I would say
I was too busy to take on the work and once you start
turning work down people don't take long to stop
asking you

True enough Licorice I haven't told you about the
job I'm starting next month. Exactly the kind of gig
I've been hoping to get and they seem keen enough on
me no doubt it helps that one of the guys is someone
I knew from college. His rise has been meteoric.
Evidently none of my carping on that score has made
its way back to him. We were in that pub when I got
the call. Waiting for our lunch. No of course you'd
buggered off with Angie and were true to form not answering your phone so Roy and me once we'd scoffed
our huge plates of food and eaten the cold chips off
yours figuring you were not going to want them were
wondering what to do no one likes to be left twiddling
their thumbs. I grabbed one of the free papers and
tried to engage him in finding a little local colour
jumble sale next Sat. exquisite bric-a-brac is that
not a contradiction in terms *lots* of home-made
produce worth underlining this week's B.O.G.O.F. at
the village shop cricket match on the village green
ooh that's timed for right after the jumble better not
tell Licorice or she'll have us all down here for the
day. Sucking up the local goodness. And I'm going
to London on Saturday how about you any plans for
the weekend? Roy sneezed. Use Licorice's napkin
it's right there mate. Well you'll have the place to

yourself if you just want to stay in bed. Yeah. That probably is what I'll do. I've got some reading to do for something I'm auditioning for chance to knock it off as long as I'm not feeling too shit. A polite fake cough behind us then. If you need something to pass the time we have board games. Rummikub. Settlers of Catan that's got so many bits to set up. Scrabble. Chess. Draughts. Operation. The kid staggered in with a pile of tatty boxes and placed them on our table. There's more if you don't like any of these. As she darted out and back again Roy followed her with his eyes. Is she angling? Shall we? Something quick. While we're hanging around for Licorice and Angela. Monopoly. Mind you I'm not sure it's got all its pieces. Dad gets me to check when they're put away some- times I find bits people have dropped when I'm cleaning up. Hope you get paid for cleaning up I said then oh yeah but not nearly enough. She laughed. The pale skin of her scalp between where her hair had been plaited into cornrows by mum big sister her godmother at a free summer festival looked so fragile. Cluedo, she said then. The body of Dr Black at the bottom of the cellar stairs. We'd be up for that okaaay so who do you want to be? I'm always Miss Scarlet, I said in my very best falsetto. Unless you want to be her. Her hand had gone up to her mouth she was shaking with laughter and her braids rattled. There you go. How about you? Why don't you choose for me, said Roy. Oh well in that case you've got to be Prof Plum cos he's the only one who looks at all like you. I'll be Colonel Mustard. Yes we sure can see him in you. Now cut the three piles of cards and put one of each no looking in the greasy murder envelope.

Shuffle the rest together and dole them out.
Colonel Mustard being the oldest gets the extra card.
Savannah! You've been told often enough not to
bother the customers. I apologise for my daughter
gentlemen really I do. That's perfectly all right
madam we were enjoying her company no I didn't say
that it was very kind of your daughter to bring over
the games. Mum I was going to be Colonel Mustard!
I already told you Savannah I need you to help me
make up the rooms upstairs. Why can't Jerry do it?
He's at football practice. He's always at bleeding
football. Okay come over here right now please. To
another occasion Colonel. Ciao, Roy said giving her a
funny little salute and the corners of her mouth lifted
in a way that made her whole face light up. A game
of chess Professor? You don't play? I am surprised

We have two days of filming left and all I can think
about is that the local dialect here had thirty different words for mud. Easier to remember in
alphabetical order clodgy gawm gubber ike pug slab
sleech slob slough slub slurry smeery stodge stug
swank all the hissing sounds someone might make
as they squelched their foot into sticky stuff and
pulled it out again. Pete sees things differently but
the story is barely there anyway, requiring so much
fleshing out we may as well be starting from scratch.
He would like to put in more hooks but really what
you're suggesting reduces Nan to a series of tropes
sexy witch well witches have been done to death
evil murderess or wrongéd maiden. I'm not having
it too many people have already been there. Those
aren't career choices Pete just lazy fucking labels:

a gross simplification of the result of a cluster of cir-
cumstances. Really what I wanted to do was to build
a time machine around this legend find out so much
relevant detail it could literally be we had turned the
clock back seven hundred years and were capturing
it on film. Getting in beautiful young people to
channel whatever they could. Angela is trying bless
her heart a little too hard ticking off all those boxes
this morning food soap sunscream and whatever.
She is not quite as confident as I expected. I'm
concerned that a lot of those on-point things she has
said to me have been what she thought I wanted to
hear. Never mind. She has really caught something
in what we've shot so far though Pete has said to me
where in the finished film is that footage of Ange in
the rain going to go exactly? Fuck you've read the
script haven't you where do you think? I also blame
myself for overdoing the attention to detail: an
obsession with textures becomes unhelpful if the
whole time you're wearing a prop you can't think
about anything except how rough and heavy it feels
next to your tender skin. That dress is not even
authentic if she'd been a proper medieval maiden
her dress would have been spun from wool grown
right up here on the chalk and dyed brilliant blue
with woad subsequently faded by years of wear.
Cloth dyed with woad doesn't even develop its full
colour until hung up in bright sunlight. But if you
don't grow the woad yourself it is fucking expensive
and my kitchen window box wouldn't have yielded
enough for a baby's sock. Ha. Would have disrupted
the colour scheme Pete and I devised in any case.
Fuck authenticity I say now it is the ultimate

illusion, a distancing mechanism to maintain
the fourth wall as the magic circle which cannot be
crossed

And is Roy just going to be sitting over there like a
big lump of wood? Coughing occasionally playing
horror games on his phone while waiting for Angela
to turn up he'd like me to think that's what he's doing
sans doute but he takes his craft very seriously ha
ha ha ha just like me. How much in the moment is
he like I'm this dude here with my sheep all around
me slept in a bush last night woke up damp chilled
covered in grass and prickles I got nowhere else to
go. When there has been so much rain for weeks the
saturated ground yields up its water on a fine clear
night with a light breeze. Wringing wet clumps of
grass droplets strung along spiderwebs adding to the
puddle of rainwater in the pond. If I was a wandering
labouring man I'd have some means of making a fire
on me to get myself warm and dry out my clothes.
I wouldn't be trying to rub two damp sticks together
always thought my time in Cubs was a waste. Of
course if Licorice hadn't banned smoking I'd have
had my trusty lighter with me. Whatever am I going
to burn these stray bits of furze heaped together
inside a circle of chalk? Licorice has told us that
we mustn't light fires up here, that the earth will be
scarred for years and nothing will grow. Imagine a
thin plume of smoke rising straight up into the sun
would she bustle over then to tick me off. Bitch has
a thermos for fuck's sake I can smell her coffee.
No thoughts of Roy has been out in the cold all night
bet he could do with a hot drink. Why thank you so

much Licorice all along you've been taking such good care of me. No treat him mean and keep him keen just do as I say and get on with it you stupid boy. None of the endless discussions of character motivation she has with Angela: of course she fancies Ange that's what a lot of this is about. And Angela for some reason is fascinated by her. When I first mentioned the Nan Kemp film my mate had gotten involved in she said she wasn't interested in such a freaky horrible story but as soon as I mentioned Licorice it was like a light bulb switched on inside her skull

Sometimes it seems to me because I know her best that Angie is flirting with Licorice but if Licorice is picking this up she's ignoring it because she doesn't want anything to interfere with making her film. Or Angie's just doing it to show me how much she really doesn't care about me. I'm not making any excuses for having fucked Elaine it was stupid I have been really fucking paying for that though Angie evidently isn't satisfied yet. A few nights ago I really needed to get to sleep early and Pete, having said he was staying up to experimentally grade what he had shot that day, burst into the lounge woke me up offered me a drink poured himself a large whisky from the bottles stash underneath his turntable and after he'd downed the first and poured himself a second glass blurted out to me that he has slept with Licorice. Twice. Like that's more likely to make me believe him. She's a real goer in my experience the older ones often are. His face going red. Can you imagine? Whatever dude. Surely if you say. Just let me go back to sleep I've pulled my eyemask back on since your curtains are so fucking thin. Sly cunt. Trying to make it seem less tragic that he's so fixated on my ex. Pete hasn't got a chance with Angie she doesn't even like him and it's not in a way that might suddenly flip over into love, she's not, because I know her, actually in denial about any kind of attraction. Pete would like to think so. But I don't think he really does

The pond as skymirror was that something you read Licorice reeds or rushes what's the difference three rubber bands dropped by the postman that I gathered up wondering until I realised they must have been around the sandwiches of people who stopped to picnic at the pond. Sheep whoa there you crazy creatures don't quit looking at me I'm filming you. Young ones because they haven't been sheared the distinctive patches of dye on their rumps out of shot until they start to scramble over each other's backs. Where the fuck are you Angela. This is crazy. It's been eight minutes since Pete texted me so it's looking like he'll be here before our leading lady. Has something happened to her? Has she got carried away filming herself and produced some amazing footage in which case everything is forgiven.... But what if she's slipped on the wet grass? She might have been so intent on filming herself that she caught her foot in a rabbit hole and is lying there watching it swell up purple with a sprain. In that eventuality wouldn't she be yelling out for help? I take off my headphones and listen. Have I gone deaf? Is it like when I forget how to breathe part of my body going into suspended animation? The breeze ruffles the grass too gently for a susurration. When I concentrate I can unpick the

sound of the dual carriageway down below a train
is heading south along the railway yeah Doppler
effect but this is taking me away from the moment:
in Nan's time where we are now was the main road
inland from the sea. And she's not coming that way.
She's landward. But wait I can hear her singing.
Oh god I hope it is her not one of the early dog walkers. The last thing I need is some overfriendly pooch
launching itself at me. What are you doing in the
bushes. We're from the uni. Doing a nature observa-
tion just make up a case reference with at least eleven
digits including two forward slashes was what Pete
suggested if we were challenged and I'm not even sure
he was joking. But if Angie comes trotting along in
her shift dress and bare feet now what is a dog walker
going to think? No no this can't simply happen clash
of worlds. Mad girl wandering on the hill would they
look at her bruised feet the dark shadows beneath
her gleaming eyes and ask are you lost my dear are
you hurt whatever's wrong? And where she's got
herself into that headspace as either Nan or Angela
would she start spinning on her tippytoes a scream
of incoherent syllables issuing forth from her mouth
the dog walker at that point turning and fleeing or
if they were made of sterner stuff grabbing her arm
and slapping her face to bring her down from what
they imagined to be some kind of hysterical fit. Or
would she just be switched-on Angie, able to fire off
some quip like you've caught me doing penance for
my sins ha ha no actually I've left off my shoes because
I have terrible problems with my feet and walking
barefoot is supposed to strengthen them. I say just
look at that woman skulking in the bushes. She

follows me around why you'd be doing me the biggest
favour if you could perform a citizen's arrest on her.
She's the reason your noble hounds are barking like
crazy after all no one should be lying in a gorse bush
by the public highway filming everything that goes
on. What business do you have being here with your
camera my good woman? Invading the privacy of
these fine upstanding law-abiding citizens and their
pets. WPC Lorelei's number is on the community
board at the bottom of this path I can rustle it up if
it's not already on your speed dial

I heard Roy sneeze then funny how I've almost
forgotten he was here just waved at him when I came
up here and got myself into position. He waved back
echoing or mirroring my gesture would you even say
that and could you do both at the same time? I haven't
given him enough thought. I know that now. When he
is even more of a made-up character than Nan when
we don't even have a name for him there is nothing to
remember him by except what is presented as a
passive part in the story he is her victim as much as
their children are and there is no sense in the legend
as it has come down of any other part he may have
played. What am I expecting him to do when Nan
comes up to the ponds? I think of Pete's words that he
will do something unexpected and I hope so but will
it be something that is intended to piss either me
or Angie off. Would he let his feelings about Angie
play out in this role. I hope not but who am I kidding
it would give a frisson: the chemistry between them
still palpable even if it's totally messed up. Angie
was voluble this morning when I was expecting her

to be quiet and I would have liked her to be quiet because I was wanting to prepare myself for this. To make myself feel completely empty, so I could just be the eyes of the camera and receive whatever happened in front of me. But she just kept talking about her preparation and the research she'd been doing and I felt that I had to be receptive and encouraging because the reason she was talking so much is she is really really nervous. Both because she wasn't sure what she was meant to do though I hope she's worked that out on the way up the hill but also because she's going to be filming with Roy and though they've been in the same space every day for the last couple of weeks they have barely spoken to each other. In the end I brushed her off with a little tough love it's not going to help you Angie to keep running over all this in your head. A conversation with Pete while I was packing stuff back into my bag and she thought not listening. Like you could have told me and Pete replying I don't know what was stopping you phoning him. You still have his number. Couldn't you have phoned him before last night if you wanted to talk to him that much? Do you think I asked him why he wanted to sleep out at the ponds? Would you have expected me to ask you that if you'd suddenly announced it. Do you think Licorice would have asked you why? Oh no wait a minute of course she would. She'd have plumbed every angle of your motivation. And why would that be exactly? She should trust you more. I trust Roy. I trust you too Angie as an actor I know you're capable of delivering a great performance

No one said anything about getting naked in the
bushes Licorice Licorice look at me sometimes I
dream about Angie calling my name and sometimes
Pete but never Roy he's never engaged with me that
directly oh here is Angie coming along the path and
what is she singing Licorice Licorice can't catch
me here I am girl over here now flitting like a sprite
or a flibbertigibbet look at me fucking girlpower I'm
going to take this motherfucker down what is he
even doing here by the pond so pretty and handsome
with his eyes of blue and skin tanned by the hot
sun or is it some expensive fake tan you've rinsed
yourself with in our mouldy second floor shower.
In his birthday suit without a stitch on looking like
some young girls' X-rated dream he's a stud of the
uplands showing off all his muscles pure Hollywood
alien this is so fucking wrong. No wonder Nan looks
so shocked. She takes a step towards him. She
doesn't know what to do. Is it Nan or Angie reacting
like this. Look at his eyes. Fucking focus. What's he
doing. Is it actually Roy in there or has he convinced
himself he's some wandering shepherd lad with an
undisclosed intent. Where she has come through the
barbed wire the dress is torn and there is blood on
the front where she has hurt her hands and wiped
them. She is in the crux of a moment there get it good
on the camera where she can go either way. Her face
is so puzzled. Her expression is not reflected in
Roy's. He looks calm and he smiles at her and in his
smile there are all sorts of things but how to pick
through them how to decipher them he doesn't say
anything to her what could he say how do you do
young maiden or remember what you're missing girl

words are completely redundant here who talks at a
time like this it's all about the image the image needs
to become somehow totally fucking transparent
like it's pushing aside layers of cloud and landscape
and all those things you might be able to feel, it just
sucks them all into itself, consumes them and what
comes out the other side something that is absolutely
indescribable. Angie's face. Nan's face. Struggling
with expressions. I cannot tell which is acting or
indeed if any of them are. They follow each other so
quickly. There is remorse and lust and horror and
love and intrigue and curiosity folding each other
round like they are the corners of a napkin no more
fucking metaphors if you can't actually show what
the camera's showing here then just forget it. Forget
that moment when you think Angie is about to strip.
She has her hand on the breast of her dress. Briefly
tugging up her hemline to reveal above her knees then
she lets it fall and seems frozen for a moment. The
other hand reaches out to touch Roy's arm. He's still
got that fucking Nicorette patch on. For a moment I
think she's going to laugh. For a moment I think she's
going to kiss him. And I can really not tell and I don't
actually care if either or both of them has any idea
that they are acting or whether what they are meant
to be doing has completely left both their minds. If
she took her dress off what would have happened
next? Would they actually have fucked there by
the pond and who would it have been fucking, Roy
and Angela or Nan and Thomas we're not showing
that scene not because I'm a prude Pete but how
can you shoot a rape scene in a way that's not going
to titillate some sick puppy. So what stopped her

then what broke the spell was it that wavering
of intent remembering that she might be acting in
a film but this was her ex-boyfriend from whom she
had moved on so thoroughly as she had told me in
such reassuringly expansive detail that she could
even feel sorry for him that he was having such a bad
time. Crossed lines with the shepherd boy, evil or
innocent whichever he might be, that her character,
the innocent or monstrous girl had just come across.
Or did she just think shit we are in a public place
on a public path and it's not so early in the morning
that people aren't going to be coming along on such
a beautiful day and if they see us naked and fucking
fucking Pete is going to be here in a minute and if
he sees us naked and fucking he's going to be filming
us too oh fuck fuck fuck

Licorice you witch how could you do this to me. You
set me up you betrayed me humiliated me don't know
what I'm talking about I'll show you what you've done
tell him to get his fucking clothes back on that's up
to him I'm not going to order him around you tell him
Angie if it bothers you you were filming the whole
thing weren't you I want to see it I want to destroy it
I'm really not going to be happy with you using that
footage why because it exposes your most innermost
feelings I don't see as it's any of your business of
course it is this is my film after all that footage is
pure gold Angie I'll show it to you when you've calmed
down and you'll agree with me but I'm not giving you
the camera now cos you'll just delete it and ruin the
whole thing. No. I don't agree. It's not your decision.
Are you not going to consult Roy. It doesn't matter

to me Angela, Roy said then but even though he'd
pulled on his briefs she was not responding to his
gaze, as far as I'm concerned Licorice and Pete
can do with the footage whatever they like. He blew
his nose. If we're finished up here I'm going to get the
bus back into town and have a shower and breakfast.
He turned away to start folding up his sleeping
bag. Angie's hands balled into fists. Your fucking
breakfast! Is that really all you're thinking about
right now? Pure frustration scratch on her face
beading blood where she had clambered through
the wire. She chucked the phone to the ground and
stamped on it, smashing the screen on the second
impact. I saw Licorice wince. Your fucking phone.
Well tough however much you paid for it. I'm not
going to show you what I shot. You'll never see it.
At least I can destroy that. You'll never know how
fucking amazing it was it would have been the
heart of your fucking film. Whatever you have will
be hollow without it. She grabbed a lump of chalk
and flint at the edge of the pond and used that to
hammer the phone into the ground. Fuckity fuck fuck
fuck. Then she tossed it right into where the gorse
bushes were thickest. She had a good aim on her and
I recollected randomly that she had 'fessed up about
being captain of her school netball team and she was
really crying, not weeping prettily but blubbering so
tears seemed to be coming out of her mouth and nose
as well as her eyes

Licorice was circling Angie at what she evidently
considered a safe distance. She was cradling her camera in her arms and obviously did not want to give

Angie the chance to get hold of it in case she destroyed that too. I couldn't tell if she was still filming. Oh there you are Pete. Late to the party as usual. Give me your fucking car keys. I've got to get dressed haven't I. No no one's coming down with me. I'll leave the keys on the fucking dashboard. And you'd better make sure you're not still at the bus stop when I get there Roy. I've had it. I've completely fucking had it with all of you. Licorice can fill you in on what's been going on. Bloody emotional rapist that's what you are you bitch fucking vampire abuser you'd steal my soul if you could to put in your film.

nononono we're never going to stop laughing long enough to film this. You wanna try again? Once more then Angie action. Just keep walking towards the ruined building and when you get there sit down on the nearest of the walls and clasp your belly like you're thinking about what's inside. Oh god looks like you're giving birth to cushion baby right here and now is the little fucker breech or oh dear. You think your waters have broken ha ha? Let's just take some stills for reference on my phone. If you sit on the wall Ange you can plump cushion baby up. He'll be resting on your thighs. Imagine your cushion baby has hiccups. That's right, have a really good laugh. Cushion baby will feel you laughing. Put your hands on him now. Think about soothing his hiccups oh lovely just keep stroking. Then think about why you're here. Turn your head slowly and focus on the spot where we emptied the charcoal from the bbq. Just a little smile. I'm going to start walking towards you. Lovely. Deep in thought there Ange. Twinge of sciatica down your right leg so shift your bum. Shooting over your shoulder now to catch you in profile looking at the ashes. And again. What is your expression now exactly? Great. Okay turn away. Stretch up a little then slump. Feels like cushion baby is kicking you in the back. Hug the little bastard. You've got it. Real sense of the space he's taking up. Now I'm going to photograph you cradling cushion baby in profile you can go as vanity fair on me as you like

It's September now and I still haven't booked my flight. If I hadn't felt I was on such a timer everything might have turned out very differently. But then if I hadn't been so pressed for time I would never have gotten Pete onboard and that *might* have meant I never actually started filming: instead *Living Chalk* (Pete pursed his lips but I challenged him to come up with a better title) would have remained a beautiful, mysterious thing in my head that I would be doing more and more research for in a bid to completely inhabit. Well it's too late for regrets. I went for broke. Angela is never speaking to me again. I phoned her that afternoon to say I was sorry but she has blocked my number and unfriended me anywhere we were in contact. She knows apologies are easy. She's no fool. Feeling you've been suckered is never pleasant. And while I had no idea Roy was planning to get all his kit off it wasn't as if I did anything to intervene once he was standing there bollock naked. I felt it was kind of a stroke of genius on his part if also a fucking disaster. Angela's encounter with Roy at the pond revealed that she wasn't as over him as she had told me and that must have been a mortifying, bitter pill for her to chew. Is it fair that — as she has told me at great and creative length — she blames me? Meet me one more time Angela to give me a chance to explain. Fuck you Licorice I'd rather throw myself in the sea. How she has got under my skin then maybe anyone who'd filled the role of Nan would

I'm not going round to her flat. I don't want her calling the police on me. I thought about walking down her street but that too could be interpreted as stalking. However there was nothing to stop me having break-fast in a café on her route to work. Eggs bacon fried bread sausage mushrooms and hash browns I never cook at home so why not I had my sketch book with me and all the time I was thinking about Angie and Roy too a little bit I was drawing with half an eye on the window and it was mostly scenes from the film with odd twists here and there, things that Pete and I hadn't actually filmed but wished we had. Nan and Thomas. Up at the pond. I've a thick jacket back in the car if I put it on I can crawl into the gorse and try and find your phone? No leave it be. For the sheep and for the birds. Give future archaeologists something to puzzle over. Gonna be so fucked and even if we retrieve the memory card Angela's not giving us permission to use whatever she shot. Gotta look on the bright side at least she won't be taking a co-director credit. Angela's footage *stays* lost there's no point worrying about it now and in any case Pete maybe we've been saved a lot of embarrassment imagine she was convinced it was really good and we just thought when we viewed it that it was a load of crap and didn't want to include it. That would have pissed her off properly. I knew I sounded hard. But there was no good in crying over spilt milk. It didn't matter, I assured him, because I could fill in the gaps with drawings as I had previously suggested and then there were always landscape shots, shots of the pond itself or a sheep stuck in the gorse, the handle of Thomas's crook resting suggestively, dusty bedraggled interiors with spoken word over them or edited into a rhythm where their duration became the film because we were seeing them through the characters' eyes. Motes of sunlight no I mean motes of dust in sunlight is that what I mean filming time

passing is a really underrated practice capture
time in an infinite fucking loop make it your own put
it away in a place where it is unassailable. Not like
memory because memory plays you false. Is that Ange
walking past the window in the very striking three-
quarter length red coat she has her collar pulled up
and her hair is wet even though she's holding an
umbrella over herself so it's from her morning shower
she's got earbuds in looks like she is practising
her French her lips moving just a fraction all those
strange words piped directly into her skull still it's
hard to see all this detail in literally the blink of
an eye when rain is running down the outside and
condensation is forming on the inside of the window

So Angie was shaken but undeterred by her fleeting
exposure to Roy's booty. Briefly knocked off course
but back on track for Paris. *Sometimes I think
England is fucking finished.* If she speaks true
where on earth does that leave me? As for Roy's
feelings I have no idea. When did the idea of getting
naked in that scene occur to him was it simply
because he was wet and cold already in the dew after
his night without a groundsheet? His sleeping bag
and clothing soaked through no solace of a fire. Did it
just seem more straightforward to strip himself bare
and was what he was presenting to Nan or Angela
meant to be complete vulnerability demonstrating he
had nowhere to fucking hide. Or was he the abuser
waylaying the young girl, flashing his bits at her in a
secluded spot? Some commitment to his role no that's
not funny since he had such a rotten cold. I realised
afterwards his teeth were chattering and all his male

parts were shrivelled up with cold not seemingly
much of a threat. What did he think when she was
standing there in front of him? Who was uppermost
in his mind at that point; Roy or Thomas? Even if
I could pump him full of truth serum I wouldn't trust
his answer. Was he thinking to soften Angela's tender heart

I didn't see Roy again after that day. Pete said he suddenly announced he was going to stay with a friend
in London and upped and left. I had a charming
and I assumed deeply insincere email apologising
for his abrupt departure what a pleasure it had been
to work with me and he was sure Pete and I would
keep him up to date with whatever happened to the
film. Oh sure. How much side has Roy got exactly?
Never underestimate an idiot or perhaps just don't
assume they're an idiot in the first place. He's your
friend. Did you think he was playing a part the whole
fucking time? Moping after Angela. Do you know
who he's staying with in London, I went on, male or
female? You're sounding very old-fashioned Licorice.
Too late to start apologising for that ha ha ha. You
didn't ask? Why would I ask? You're glad he's gone?
Pete shrugged. I wouldn't say glad though if you'd
asked me a week ago that is *exactly* what I would have
said. But no. I certainly notice he's not there. You
miss him then? You're not going to be lonely as long
as I'm around till we've got the film finished I'm not
giving you a moment's peace. I miss both of them,
Pete replied. You know I came to enjoy the way Angie
would beetle her brows at me? Not as sharp on the
comebacks as she'd have liked to be but those scowls

oh man. And how about you Licorice? Your little puppets. Wouldn't let it lie would you Pete

Watching through what we'd managed to shoot it was
great, it was really really good but there was not very
much of it. I'd pinned my hopes on the scene at the
pond bringing it all more into focus but though Pete
didn't say anything I could see hot mess was right
there at the forefront of his thoughts. I mean I do
actually agree with you, he said when I prodded him,
that we couldn't have shot that scene the way I would
have liked to. What might have worked however
he slid me another careful look would have been to
have a couple more cameras set up. Automatically
recording in the gorse to capture it from alternative
vantage points. Then at least there would have been
backup footage. For a bit of experimental cutting
to make it more dynamic. It's very *still* he drew the
word out when you're filming. Apart from where I'm
climbing out of the bush to try and get the fucking
angle as they move away and almost take a nosedive.
Yeah. I mean the same would have happened to me
motherfucking rabbit holes but also Licorice he
paused and met my eyes your camera is almost always on Angela. I mean I can't fucking believe I'm
saying this but there's really not enough of Roy. We
don't get his reaction. Angela yes we get how she
reacts and we could maybe use the footage where
she is yelling at you to stop and you're backing away
and your camera swings round then to follow Roy,
I'm not even sure if it's on purpose but he's already
walking away. It's like he finally makes it into
the film and he's hardly shrug I mean we see his

arse and his back he does glance over his shoulder when Angie screams his name so if we edit that out of the soundtrack. Pete's face is reddening I have to ask Licorice were you actually embarrassed filming him? It might have thrown me without any warning and shit I should be used to him lolling around on my sofa in his nuddypants. Why Pete you're talking like you think I've never filmed a naked guy before. Hate to break this to you but I've probably filmed way more than you have. Not proud of it but I made a few pornos some years back. And no I'm not talking about some kind of feminist porn though sure that's what it should have been with my credentials and no of course it's not under my own name it's one of the darker spots on the chequerboard of my career and no I've no idea of the titles these things have multiple titles to eke their shelf lives out a bit

You couldn't make it up. Just bloody shut up already. And no I haven't answered your question. Angela gathering firewood. Angela running up the hill. Her dress a greige blot against the etched chalk path. Twirling in the rain. Gazing thoughtfully up at the brand new windmill. I don't remember that. I don't think you were there Licorice. Perhaps you were late. Probably you and Roy and Angie were late, I said. That was more often how it was. Keep your hair on. Okay say we were late and you'd obviously been there on time and because we hadn't shown up and you'd got bored, you'd wandered off somewhere to reccy something and probably to teach us a lesson you were not answering your phone. So why is Roy not in the picture? Why do you think? I was stuck with his

79

ugly mug all the time at home. Why would I go to the trouble of filming it? Or perhaps he'd wandered off and it was just Angela standing there staring up at the windmill. What's she thinking about? I'd hazard a guess Licorice she's just spotted the security cam. The words were out of my mouth before I considered what I was saying. Fuck. To let that slip after all this time. I haven't ever noticed any cam you replied then tapping and swiping already searching home security systems on your phone. These new ones are so neat you're not meant to not the big old camera on a swivel arm at all. On a building like the mill where the surface is overlapping clinkerboards irregular angles the sweeps themselves there are plenty of places one could be tucked in. You think Ange spotted one above the roundhouse door keeping an eye on whoever is coming and going? Wouldn't she have said anything to us? I don't know I'm not a mind reader. She may have assumed we already knew. You didn't look up then just nodded as if agreeing that once you'd built yourself an expensive facsimile wooden windmill in an out of the way spot of course you would protect yourself against burglars vandals or the local potential pyromaniac by installing a state-of-the-art security system to monitor what was going on

What's the film quality like in these things? Fucking HD. This one claims to provide images good enough to be used in never mind. If we had zoomable HD images and sound they'd certainly be good enough for our film. She glanced at me inquiringly how I hated to rain on her parade. Licorice most of these upload the footage they record and store it remotely for a limited time. Always sounds so neat and ethereal oh look they are in the cloud see the one shaped like a huge server farm three quarters of the way to the north pole consuming more power than a small town to keep our data alive? Mmm. I think I got a handle on this now. Seven days it says here for the default so the footage with us is long gone unless. She shrugged again smiling faintly. Half of me was relieved she had plumped for this aspect to consider rather than berating me for never clueing her in about the security cam the other half was freaked out by her clutching so desperately at these fragile straws. Quicksand. I had no idea what to do. Her smile broadened as she kept scrolling down then she threw back her head and laughed. Okay so I had no idea any of this was even possible how out of date does that make me. The price tag on this curvy little robot is only three hundred quid. Shall I ask Mitzi to get one for our house Pete? Then we could just glance at a monitor and know exactly who is outside the front door without having to go all the way down the stairs no picture on the fucking intercom after all I'd install it in my own time will you chip in some dosh. No way I wanted a security system but this was a test she was waiting to jump down my throat if I put a foot wrong. Fifty quid I said then to get her off my back I can go to the cashpoint and get it for you now if you like. She shook her head, frowning at her phone. Facial recognition software. Ha. Biometrically so once our faces had been captured every single measurement and contour would have been rehashed into data. So they could have been

observing us every time we came and presumably
she frowned at me again because they didn't perceive
us as any kind of threat they didn't call the police
just watched us listened to us and stopped watching
when we went away down the lane. A lost movie of
our scooby gang antics Ange pointedly reading some
great classic of world literature on her phone and
telling you to fuck off on a semi-regular basis Roy
picking his nose and moaning yes I know right did
he ever myself pootering around and bossing you
all like herding frigging cats. You doing your thing.
Always looking for angles. Composing everything as
a series of stunning shots. So cool and clinical. That
perfect viewfinder in your head. Don't get me wrong
I'm grateful really I am your eye Pete balances my
messy old punk lack of aesthetic. Creepy to think
that whenever we knocked on the roundhouse door
the owners wherever they were sun-drenched beach
castle in spain or walking among vineyards reaching out to touch slowly ripening bunches of grapes
would have received a specific alert on their phones
stating subjects one two three four are back at the
mill skinny old Asian bird the man with the movie
camera the two pretty ones standing apart with their
hands shoved deep in their pockets all indie cover
art or straight out of Watteau

You don't agree? You don't remember them gam-
bolling on the swing in the children's play area on
the village green probably lucky no one shook their
fist in our face you're older than twelve and you
can't read shame on you. It's got two big swings two
baby swings like little boxes they stick their legs

through a really small climbing frame with woodchip underneath and a small horse and a giant duck the same size as the horse mounted on wobbly springs. And a bench for mums to sit on. Or teenagers having a sneaky puff. While you and I were doing all the donkey work of measuring distances checking orientations why waste Roy and Angela's precious attention span on that why don't you two just wander around and see what you think. Soak up the atmosphere. Because this is where Nan and Thomas lived. You might even find their hovel ha ha ha or you could look for the cottage you most fancy and see if you can get yourselves invited in. That's your assignment for today class dismissed. There's one for sale at the far end of the street Roy read off his phone. Shall we start there Ange? Yeah brilliant can we be looking for our weekend retreat? What's our budget Licorice? Two hundred, Pete said then. If you can find somewhere to film the interiors. Get them to show you their old outhouses stables pantries cellars. Say you want a little studio or a darkroom you don't have to be that specific. Then when you come back you can tell me and Licorice if there's anywhere that might be suitable and we'll take it from there. Just really somewhere big enough to hold the two of you. A space you can possibly imagine that you might have inhabited domestically. And before you're thinking can't we find somewhere on Airbnb and film on the fly let me assure you I have already looked. There's nowhere suitable

How do you think Nan might have looked up at this windmill if it was here in her time? If she'd walked up this lane with her sack of wheat to be turned into flour. You're young and strong it'll keep you out of trouble for the day. Walking slowly up the lane bent almost double in her faded blue dress it would have been an old one of her mum's in all probability her feet wrapped in rags she has plaited her yellow hair for once to keep it away from the sack smell of grain tickling her nose and she sneezes twice the sack threatens to slip can't let that happen. Do you remember Pete what I told you about the language of the sweeps if they are at rest in the position of a giant plus sign it means the miller will be back soon. An X means the miller has gone away. You can wait her mum had said didn't reply hope he's ages. Perch on the mill's top step everything looks tiny and moves so slowly down below can't recognise anyone they all look like insects until his wife spies me and tells me to make myself scarce she can't abide the young girls coming round. The light seems different up here nothing else in the way breeze in my hair. If it's sunny your shadow steals the sun from everyone down below. If it's cloudy we own the fucking clouds. Why Nancy you've got so tall and pretty I hardly recognised. Why don't you come up into the mill to see the stones grinding you always used to like to when you came with your dad. Bedstone and runner stone fit together snugly tentering and lightening to accommodate the varying wind speed crucial grain flows across the grooves at the correct rate. Make sure I'm not taking more than my five per cent ha ha ha. No thank you mister hands are everywhere I'll stop out here and think on my own precious thoughts

Remember that picture of the blue post mill in the Luttrell Psalter? The miller, almost the size of the mill itself, stands on the steps in front of it cradling a full sack in his arms. The woman with her head covered and her right foot on the bottom step waits to receive the sack of flour on her bent back. A dog that looks like a wolf with a heavy collar sits alertly on a stylised projection that represents the mill's tailpole. The building has windows in the shapes of a small arch and a four-petalled flower up at the top which echoes the cross of the four sweeps on the other side. Lily cowslip nothing like the keys of heaven. Might Angie be trying to work out the wind direction so if the fantackle had been in place on top of the tailpole the body of the mill could start turning? She starts to walk clockwise. When she notices you are filming her she scowls and gives you the finger. Fuck you Pete, she says. Have I got my fucking costume on? So you turn off the camera. Black screen. You don't remember what happened after that? Probably Roy came back or you tripped into view saying good news everyone! Let's go for a walk in the rain and I'll tell you all about something else jolly interesting. I am teasing you

Actually that day it was unpleasantly cold because Angela is wearing her bright blue fleece. When she was certain I'd switched the camera off — I'd made a big show of putting it back in its bag and slinging it over my shoulder so she could be in no doubt that I had stopped filming her — she paused at the door of the windmill's roundhouse. I was still watching her but she was basically ignoring me. She had spotted something stuck in the letter box. Not obvious from where I was standing but that letter box has such a strong fingernipping spring as you and I have found out to our cost. Angie must have noticed a corner of paper sticking out because very carefully with her left hand if I remember correctly she pushed and held in the flap of the letter box as far as she could while with her right index finger and thumb she tugged it free. From the way it was folded Licorice it was one of your drawings that hadn't quite made it down to the mat. Angela would scarcely have troubled herself to look at one of my notes. So there she was carefully unfolding your bit of paper and smoothing it out against the knee of her jeans and she stood looking at it for quite some time. I couldn't see her face but her whole attitude was intense. You remember that look of hers don't you? She was probably figuring out what it was meant to be since the corner outside the flap had gotten soaked with rain and I always use India ink, as you've commented, Pete, so moisture seeping through the paper's fibres dilutes each line into a smear a smudge. An evolution of meaning that's how I like to think of it ha ha ha what a shame you weren't filming her at that point. Oh so either I'm filming her when she doesn't want to be filmed or not filming her when you think it would have been a good idea. Shafted either way. If Angela frowned when she looked at the drawing was it because of what she saw or what she couldn't see. Hmmm. Or maybe the ink was coming off on her fingers

If I never asked you what the drawings were Licorice it was because I always figured you knew what you were doing. Would you have liked me to tell you Pete? I'll tell you a crazy thing now if you like. Of course you know what a zoetrope is? A circus ring, held on a stick, with peepholes all round its enclosing wall. On the inside is drawn a sequence of say a horse running or a man jumping: when you spin the zoetrope and squint through the slits the pictures inside appear to move. A primitive form of animation. You've guessed it haven't you? The mill is my fucking zoetrope. If I had the power I would get the drawings to fly up on the walls, just like that, in the exact right order. She clicked her fingers. Very sorcerer's apprentice, the bit at the start where everything is going so well and the apprentice is cock-a-hoop that he has set all these things in motion and they are doing his bidding. Before he twigs that the things he has set in motion are no longer under his control and it's all just fucking chaos ha ha. And then the mill would turn — if the fantackle was in place on its tailpole, spinning faster and faster and anyone standing outside and looking through the cracks would see our film playing. Imagine that if you will Pete. Gathering momentum after a few minutes it might not even be visible at all

We'll open on a black screen who says that's not going to work. I'm all in favour, we've discussed this, of making a virtue of lacunae but it's a lot harder when there's barely anything in between. I keep thinking of things we should have done which would have guarded against this eventuality: I could have recorded Ange and Roy reading — anything really — stories out of the local paper lists of dialect words it wouldn't have mattered they couldn't pronounce them right. Or I just wish I'd had my phone on to record sometimes when they spoke. You know the unexpected stuff people come out with which would in retrospect have been great for the film but once they've said it and the words have gone you can't really say hang on a minute just turn back time and say it again with exactly the same impression of your thoughts tumbling sweetly into place. Half the time they wouldn't recollect what they'd said and you'd see their puzzled eyes trying to work out what the fuck it was I thought was so great. Once Angie said apropos of nothing she thought the road — the B whatever it is forming half of the crossroads where Nan met her end — was sinking. At the time I just smiled and squeezed her hand. She was in a state anyway remember the one time we went to the village pub? Perhaps I didn't ask her what she meant because I guessed her explanation would not accord with my thinking: as it was Angie saying the road was sinking seemed to fit in perfectly with something I'd been trying to put my finger on. At that time I still couldn't quite get it, and to try to verbalise it, to ask her what she actually meant, would have damaged my own fragile concept. Sinking. What is that all about. When all other indicators hint at a slow process of accretion. There are ferns they've been really going for it in the rain all along the sides of the boundary walls and at the top of the walls are masses of bristling spindly trees, simultaneously stretching up to and blocking out the light. None of them look old. But if you wandered in that wood at the side of the road not that there is a footpath it is private ground you might notice the remnants of old coppice stools. Some of them could date back almost to Nan's time

A story I came across the other day reminded me that the section of road including the crossroads where Nan was hanged is known as the hollow. It's a great story Pete if I'd seen it earlier I might have tried to make it part of the script and even so I'm wondering if we could deploy it as a kind of coda, perhaps if you read it out let's see what you think. It makes a change from all those stories of kids courting death beneath the wheels of a speeding car by dancing round Nan's grave on Halloween waiting for the witch to appear. This takes place a hundred and forty years ago. A male voice describes coming across a family party trying to build themselves a shelter by the side of the road just outside the town. The parents and three young children have two trained bears and a white pony alongside. A police-man is telling them they must move on and several people, not all unsympathetic to the strangers, have gathered to observe. The narrator offers to pay their night's lodging in a hostelry to which the policeman replies he can't allow the bears to enter town. One of the passers-by suggests the hollow as a quiet place where the family could set up camp and the narrator takes it upon himself to escort them thither. The father of the family addresses him in French. They are originally from Bosnia but have been travelling through France with the performing bears for several years. Since they got off the ferry they had been harried from pillar to post, never allowed to camp by the side of the road because someone always comes along to move them on. When the narrator asks what drew them to England they answer they had heard it was a better country than France. He advises them to head back across the Channel but they have no money for the return trip. He leads them up the track from the town and I guess there would have been an iron bridge across the railway then but the huge cutting for the road would not she shrugged have been made for another eighty years so where the concrete bridge that spans it all now is would have been solid ground. Up through the wood and past the original windmill to this bit of road that sinks down, as Angie said that day, where Nan is buried, because he describes it as a quiet bit of road no one goes along at night and Nan as a poor wretch who would have no objection to her fellow outcasts camping there. But no sooner had they arrived and were setting up camp and starting a fire to cook the children some food than a man popped his head up over the hedge and said they must move on. He was leading a party with guns into one of the neighbouring fields and said they could shoot no rabbits if the family were camped in the hollow. While the narrator was arguing with him, trying to persuade him to let the family stay the night, the mother and father with a bear on a leash apiece and the white pony led by the eldest girl with the two younger children clinging to its back set off up the road over the hill you know that's the very path we took Pete up past the ponds and the narrator says they became lost to his sight

So what happens next Licorice? Are you telling me
this as some kind of oblique comment on your own
plight when you won't ever answer any of my questions? Am I just meant to nod like I totally get it and
leave you in peace? I can't see its relevance to the film
you originally planned and feel stupid I don't dare tell
you this just shrug in a non-committal way. There
are so many things we're not talking about right now.
Shall we start with my car? Shall we reveal why even
if a space comes free right in front of the house I'm
not going to park there? Once upon a time I would
have been ecstatic at the prospect of not having to lug
all my gear halfway down the next street but now I'm
not thinking about that kind of thing at all. I haven't
used my car since the day we filmed up at the ponds.
I'm not going to use it again even though you point out
to me with some irritation that you've deepcleaned
it ultrathoroughly just as you promised. It smells of
disinfectant and upholstery shampoo but underneath
all that I think I can detect the smell of Angie's blood.
Not blood metal is what you can smell it is a car isn't
it? So don't pull this Lady Macbeth stunt on me Pete
why zounds and gadzooks Licorice I can't imagine
what you mean. It is blood from a minor injury, you
repeat, it's not like anyone has died in your car. If you
cut your hand and got blood all down your favourite
shirt would you throw it away without even trying to
clean it? Wasteful but then I suppose men do make
such a fuss about blood. Angie is absolutely fine as I
told you I've seen her no not spoken with her you must
be joking. She's never willingly coming near either
of us ever again. And honestly Pete no way is she
thinking about your car. She's moved on we need to

My poor little car. Even if Angela's handprint was no longer visible on the back of the driver's seat I couldn't forget it. As soon as I strapped myself in under Licorice's eagle eye and reached for the ignition I felt like Angie's fingers were shoving me hard in the back. I got out of the car and went back into the house without a word to Licorice. There was definitely stuff I needed to come to terms with but for the moment can we just put all of it on hold. A whole forest of magic trees no of course I wouldn't hang them all up most would be tucked away inconspicuously still throwing out their powerful scent. New car daisy fields black ice twisted basil bold embrace what the fuck I put a sign in the car window offering it for sale. Just a couple of hundred pounds. Probably not that cheap. The car didn't look great even before Angie wreaked her vengeance on it on the other hand it started reliably every time. In some ways I'm relieved I haven't had any enquiries because the thought of someone looking over the car makes me very nervous. I just want shot of it now. I wish I could bring myself to leave my keys in the ignition surely it wouldn't be long before someone took advantage and drove off. Joyriding kids but wherever they abandon it it would be traced back to me. Even if I drove out into the countryside again and set it on fire my name would come up on the DVLA database just what we want a burly policeman knocking at the door about the burned out wreck or maybe a return visit from those two community support officers with their bizarre questions about how safe I actually feel living in this neighbourhood

When we eventually got back to my car after the shoot up at the ponds it looked like a crime scene. Ange had left the keys on the dash as promised but she'd turned everything upside down the car's contents were strewn all over the grass. Had she forgotten where she left something had we carelessly dumped our crap on top of her clothes was this an act of vengeful despoliation you tell me Licorice. Instead you started wombling around picking up little bits of crap because as long as you were looking at the ground you weren't having to meet my eyes. I checked the rest of my equipment in the boot but that thankfully Angela hadn't touched. The only thing she'd left in the car was the dress she had worn as Nan it lay scrumpled on the back seat and shit there was a bloody handprint on the back of the driver's seat where she had rested her hand scrambling in. Not an accident she'd scumbled it from side to side working her blood into the fabric like I was never meant to get it out. I managed to turn away before throwing up. Just water in my stomach but I kept on retching until it felt like acid. Froth on the buttercups then you were standing in front of me are you alright Pete oh sure once I managed to get my breath how about you? For the first time since I'd known you you'd taken out your ponytail so your long black hair fell either side of your face and there was grey mixing in. You raised your camera and took a picture of my spittle on the yellow flowers. Don't take my photo Licorice. Okay Pete. Did Angela leave the dress? Yes it's right there in the middle of the back seat I haven't touched it

You photographed the dress several times, zooming in to get extreme close-up, walking round to the other side of the car, climbing into the passenger seat and shooting from there. Oh and from above the back window. I didn't say anything. You weren't so much photographing the dress as the memory of Angela inside it where she had cast it off like some sort of fucking chrysalis did you think the fabric was damp with her blood and sweat and tears and might still retain a little of her warmth? Or were you playing forensic photographer at the crime scene. Cool and collected professional steady hands no longer shaking like when you tried to shoot more footage up at the ponds head in hands I've deleted it you do it Pete bloody gorse half-heartedly. Roy sitting on the grass not saying anything watching us both giving Angela plenty of time to get herself sorted out and catch a bus. No mate. You're not filming me any more. Any coffee left in your thermos Licorice? As he rummaged through her bag split shadows thorns fucking hell sitmat more tissues can I have these energy bars? Whatever Licorice just said. So I'm gonna walk back now guys. Carefully zooming in on the messy handprint. Measuring it. This is totally freaking me out. Watching you gravely perambulate the car all I can think is that molecules of Angie Allardyce's DNA are all over it and I hope desperately but with to be honest instincts at peak selfish she is safely back at home because if anything at all has happened to her on the way then the police are going to be examining my car and what but the most horrible conclusions would they draw

You set down your camera on the grass and reach
for the dress clasping it tenderly awkwardly like you
are worried about holding it the wrong way. Your
arms sag as if under a much greater weight as you
crush the dress to your chest and bury your face in
it are you inhaling Angela and is this erotic stop.
Then you bunch the cloth up between your fingers
and I wonder if you're thinking of Angela or Nan.
The dress as a baby shawl the dress as a bloody clout
Nan used to hide their butchered limbs and is this
what you're channelling, swaying gently from side to
side, you know in medieval times people walked on
the balls of their feet as their shoes didn't have built
heels they didn't push forward from the back like
we do today. Was that so Licorice. Not just bare feet,
bloodied and bruised. We could have taken her shoes
up to the pond why did neither of us think of that
what kind of monsters are we? Were you expecting
me to be filming you? In a way I wanted to but at the
same time I absolutely couldn't face it. I was im-
agining that if I picked up the camera you would I
didn't know what you'd do having the camera on
you there you might start keening and wailing like
a banshee. And could we have used that in the film
or would you just have turned your back to me or
screamed at me to stop. We could have used that too.
Pete, you say then, have you got a plastic bag for
this? What are you planning to do with it Licorice?
You shrug in a way that could mean you have no idea
what you are going to do with the dress more likely no
intention of telling me and I don't press you

You will have drawn it into your log book for starters.
Would you have neatly arranged it on a coathanger
or just let it lie where you tipped it out of the plastic
bag? Or might you have chucked the bag in the trash
and drawn it from memory. Surrounded by notes
and observations which I imagine filling the whole
page in your tiny writing, where exactly once you'd
begun were you going to stop? Turning the book once
you'd filled the page and writing over it at ninety
degrees. That's what letter writers used to do when
postage was charged at so much a sheet you once
said. Not back in Nan and Thomas's time you added
chances are they would both have been functionally
illiterate. Words for them faded on the air hold
your tongue or spew out your most random thoughts
language is purely an interface with sensation no
tender sweet nothings or ill-intentioned promises
coming back to bite. Writing meaning into oblivion
or perhaps you just dipped your brush in the inkwell
and blackwashed that whole page. That was when
you'd locked yourself into your room and weren't
answering your door. I'm busy Pete go away. I've
got a headache. I don't feel like working today. I'm
too depressed to get out of bed. If you'd said any of
those things I could at least have engaged with you
but as it was you preserved a silence which might
have convinced me if I hadn't known better that you
had actually gone out. But where you gonna go to
Licorice? The inside of your head is a strange place.
All those films that never got made. The effect on
your daily life of thinking at any moment it could be
interrupted. When you're living from hour to hour
no break that down to minutes in your current state,

you lose track of time and the moment feels per-petually compromised. You don't have a bank card any more. You say that is because your income is not regular enough and you don't want to have that temptation to spend extravagantly when you know you would struggle to pay it back. All very sensible but less than half true. You fear being tracked by the purchases you make either in shops or online. A couple of times you have asked me to buy things for you and given me the money in cash. I'm cool with that. Where does the cash come from? Not my business. You never ask me about what's going on in my life apart from our film. I keep saying I've got a new job coming up so from next week I'll be working in London but do you ever take it in? I had assumed our film would be done and dusted by then. I mean when we have so little to go on how much more can there be to fucking do

Sometimes I wonder Licorice if this whole thing about your status here is some kind of fantasy you have gotten incredibly wrong. Maybe you are not in imminent danger of being deported at all it has just come to seem that way to you. Or your status can be fixed quite straightforwardly by filling in a few simple online forms. Abracadabra! Indefinite leave to remain. But I cannot say that to you because it would seem I don't believe anything you say. So I try to do some research but it's as clear as mud from the information I can access through government portals when I don't know in detail what your situation is. I'm going by what you've told me and that's a joke, because you have told me zilch, it's just whatever you have let slip and when I've thought about any of that it's never to any useful purpose. One bit of misinformation leads to another forming block chains forming chain mail into a spider's web of potential inferences and outcomes, a sticky swampy paranoid mess. Is any of it accurate? When you gathered that I had been looking up government portals online, trying to inform myself more about the ins and outs of your situation, you were angry. Not shouty instead you hunch up like you are concentrating your resources I hope you didn't do it from here. No I lie quickly of course not from a coffee shop in town. You peer at me through your spread fingers nails black with ink a weeping burn the size of a two pound coin on the back of your left hand how did you even do that when you don't have a cooker? They'll be thinking why is someone at that address doing that? you go on. No one is curious about such things Pete unless it affects them in some way. If it's not part of their normality they haven't got any reason to think about it

Back in time. Angela snuggled up with Roy in the back of my car head on his shoulder but nodding vaguely from time to time smell of damp leaves always more noticeable when it rained rattling drops on the roof Licorice twisting round from the passenger seat in best explainer mode. You know why there were so many windmills in this area? No running water on the chalk so watermills were never an option. Each windmill represented a major capital investment the lord of the manor or the church held a local monopoly over this method of food processing one in each village before then every farmer would have had their own set of grinding stones and these were known as blood stones very fee fi fo fum don't you think how many hours of manual turning did it take some poor skivvy to grind flour for the family loaf? Millers were frequently suspected of diverting a larger portion of the customer's grain than was their due into their own sacks hard to tell when wastage is inherent in any process of transformation flour flying up into the air huge fire hazard chaff and husks if the purest whitest flour is desired sifted out through a boulting cloth as bran. Burr stones the finest French millstones segments of quartz joined by calciferous cement and bound within an iron hoop the patterns known as harps on each contact surface have to be recut as friction wears them down to preserve the perfect scissoring action of two sets of grooves grinding opposite ways. Have you heard the expression *miller's thumb* it grew a particular shape from testing grain and flour against the palm or was it a thumb of gold added value at every turn of the sweeps the mill was a money machine no wonder they kept on building them throughout the industrial revolution. Now look at this picture on my phone guys and tell me if you have any idea at all what is happening? That is the old mill we visited yes the one with the tea and cakes being moved from its original location near the sea right up to where it stands now on the top of the Downs. A large frame has been constructed underneath the crossbeams it looks like the struts that form the rafters of the round-house are still in place they have been reinforced to hold it upright so huge and top-heavy dragged by eighty-six oxen harnessed in six rows. A one-legged

giant stalking the landscape how mad is that the
drivers goading the oxen they would have to be
carefully synchronised the timbers of the building
vibrating like crazy as it lurches over the rough
uneven ground. No wonder people have gathered to
watch. This is at the end of the eighteenth century
the women are wearing poke bonnets to keep the sun
off their delicate skin. As towns expanded they often
surrounded mills and it made no economic sense for
a mill to stay at a location where new buildings would
be interfering with the flow of wind to its sweeps.
Not to mention the new neighbours' objections to
the mill's operational noise and dust. These moves
weren't always successful sometimes the multiple
strains put on the structural timbers meant the
body of the mill collapsed into smithereens

When was it I started to think that what you were
doing with all the information all the stories every
single detail you dredged up from microblogs down
the back of the internet was generating spells and
whether you thought of them as a springboard for the
successful realisation of the film or a protective wall
of words creating headspace wherein the land could
be construed separately from the machinery of the
state that so concerned you? A witch stone with a hole
in it hung around your neck on a bit of string. Found
it on the beach such a pretty shape and who knows
when a protective amulet's gonna come in handy
ha ha. Why would anyone go to all that trouble and
expense to reconstruct the mill if it's just generating
a bit of power to feed back into the grid. I mean if
you were after bang for your buck wouldn't you just

erect a regular wind turbine? Planning objections maybe it's not anyways logical. People don't like wind turbines, I said, unless they're out at sea so far away they become tiny and silent to any but the ships wending their way in and out between the masts and my turn to overdo the information Licorice those irregular gaps you may have observed in the array mark the beds of prehistoric rivers. How cool is that. Bedazzling camouflage from the whirling blades a great spiky kinetic fortification right down the middle of the Channel

Oh people can be scared of anything. Everything in the world someone will be afraid of. Anemophobia is the fear of windmills wind turbines and even draughts and yes it is like the flower some ancient woodlands round here carpet white with wood anemones *windflowers* in early spring before the bluebells come along and the name means 'daughter of the wind' from the Greek *anemos* for wind plus *one* feminine patronymic suffix and they were called that because people thought the flowers only opened when the wind blew. Daughter of the wind that's lovely isn't it. Angie smiled then like something had very much engaged her but she didn't share and when she noticed I was observing her in the mirror she dug Roy in the ribs and he glanced at me shrugging I rolled my eyes and Angela seethed not very inwardly. Girl is cray, Roy opined weeks later when he was sleeping on my floor and I had asked him because I was sick of his stupid face why the fuck when you had Angela as your sweetie would you go screw Elaine? You don't know the half of it. Interesting that people used to talk about flowers *blowing* rather than *blooming* idea of the wind as animating breath. Why thank you Licorice for reading us all of that off of your phone. You laughed then thank you all for being so patient with me. The whirling of the sweeps. An inanimate object seeming alive. Think about it. You add with an apologetic smile the thing about Don Quixote tilting at windmills everyone already knows. Angela nods. Even Roy nods. Little puppets in unison suspended from the roof of my car. Quixote believes the windmills are giants because in the stories that define his worldview there *are* giants and windmills don't exist I say then but what in Nan's story if anything could that be true of

What you really wanted from Roy and Angela was something they could only provide off their own bat. Roy turned it out in spades at the end, completely wrongfooting Angie, and as the situation continued to disintegrate both you and myself. I only realised belatedly that brinkmanship was not your bag: what you actually wanted to do was push the whole thing off the edge of the cliff and observe what happened. Even when you're making a film with an experimental remit you don't reckon on pissing off your cast so much they disappear before filming is finished. Absolutely no point saying that to you now. I get up all the film we have shot and look at it and think about your script and how we can put this shit together so it works. There is the other footage as well, stuff I know you have on your phone I'm not talking about the Morris men and there is stuff on my phone too, even when I was looking at rough set-ups for shots which possibly we could include. Could get some interesting kind of juxtapositions, the impressions of scenes and locations emerging and dissolving. You're not going to care if the grading doesn't match and I'll go with you on that since there's no prospect of turning out anything I'd recognise as a film. The footage with the actors is much more of a problem, if we cut in shots of Roy and Angie in modern day dress then duh the story changes. Did you not just want to fuck her because she is so pretty. I mean obviously you had a thing for her not any more not after that day. You really shat on her Licorice was what I didn't add. How would you have replied? At least she's learnt not to expect anyone else to protect her. At least she realises how powerful she is

How do I feel about it now why are you bothering to ask. The various suggestions I make you pooh-pooh like I'm an idiot or worse. You dislike being photographed for all the obvious reasons. The one image I captured of you and Ange is a doozy you're sitting on the grass on one of the few really summery days and you've got your heads together that was why you didn't notice me snapping you on my phone and I think you've got something in your hand that you're showing to Angela had you picked it up off the chalk spinning her some fantabulous yarn and she is wearing a sheer white shirt with hanging sleeves over a tight black vest leaning forward with her arms clasped around her knees you have each other's full attention the way Angie smiles when she is looking at you hanging on your every word crystal glory is my ringtone floats into my head that was the moment I fixed forever answers on a postcard please. Like the time I said in a bid to lift you out of your lethargy that if it would help your situation in any way we could get married and you spent ages telling me all the reasons why it would never work and started in on my motives into the bargain so you can think you're some kind of hero that's why you say this I'm not owing anything to some boy who considers he's doing me a favour of all the things I thought you might say I mean seriously Pete. You're probably committing some offence by offering me a marriage of convenience even if you're not asking for a few grand. I've already put you in a dodgy position by being frank with you about my irregular status in the current climate if you were a better citizen you'd be turning me in. I didn't vote for this government Licorice I'm no friend of the state. That's a luxury you can afford Pete because no one's trying to send you home. You simply haven't thought this through. As soon as we went into the town hall to register our intent to marry the staff would be asking us all sorts of questions. They would be going through our paperwork with a fine toothcomb and once they'd spotted quite how expired my visa is it would be on the phone to the Borders Agency the police would be summoned and I wouldn't be allowed to leave the building before they arrested me. Once my status has been determined as irregular they're not going to let me stay just because you're prepared to marry me. You would have to come over to wherever I've been deported to and marry me there: once you'd returned to the UK you could apply for a spousal visa to bring me in but you would need to prove your income to be way higher than I imagine it is so going forward I wouldn't be any kind of drain on the British tax-payer. In any case I've blotted my copybook so thoroughly that even if we jumped through all those hoops they'd be unlikely to let me back in. It would mess up your life something rotten and it's not like we're in love air quotes or there's any kind of erotic connection between us she caught my right hand before I realised what she was doing and lifted it briefly to her lips without for a nanosecond lowering her gaze. I've shocked you yes all you're feeling is that my mouth is cold and dry. She retained my hand turning it over as if she was studying my palm. When's my birthday Pete? How old am I? Where was I born are my parents still alive what are the names of my brother and sister my birth name even where and when did we first meet have you already forgotten was what I didn't get a chance to say how about my favourite food? Easy peasy fish and chips I interjected in a bid to regain some of the increas-ingly shaky ground no no no Pete you're wrong she glared that is treat food it's not my favourite it's not what I eat to sustain me every day don't go thinking despite the circs of us living in the same house that you actually know anything about me

Tomorrow I am due to start the new job in London. I had persuaded myself we owed it to Ange to look at the footage she took going up the hill demonstrating her total autonomy with no interference from anyone else and if I looked at it even though we weren't going to use it which Licorice had always made it clear she was dead against I might be able to flesh out and

rebalance the narrative we had shot. Who was
I kidding this was my last chance to indulge my own
curiosity. Enemy interference on the way up the hill
from the kind of posh English bird who thinks she's
so fucking entitled daddy and mummy have provided
everything and she was standing there on the steep
white path with her horse, hanging onto its bridle
for grim death there was foam on the horse's lips and
it was struggling to get away from her. Immediately
above the path brown ponies with black manes and
tails milled around snorting and whinnying why the
fuck were they there? You'd probably told us at some
stage when I wasn't paying attention. Tight jodhpurs
and her boots shiny where they weren't hazed with
chalk dust. Thick blonde hair tucked into a net under
her hard hat. Quick. Can't you do something. Throw
stones at them. No way darling. Throw your own
stones if you have to. For fuck's sake I'm not asking
you to try and hit them, I'm asking you to scare them
away because they're scaring my horse. Are you not
going to help me? I'm going to have to let him go if he
keeps pulling like this and I don't know what they'll
do or he's going to hurt himself. Because I thought
that otherwise I was never going to get past her up
the path, I took a step towards the ponies and yelled
at them, waving my arms and they flurried back a
little which somehow allowed the girl to drag her
horse down the path though it was fighting her and
snorting every centimetre of the way its hooves
slipping and sparking on flints in the chalk. In fact
the horse nearly knocked me over as it went past and
I can only assume it was because she didn't notice
that she didn't apologise

Grass on grass always greener after rain you said
that is full of dissolved nitrates threatening the
balance of this fragile ecosystem not enough sheep
to crop it close before it outcompetes rare chalkland
plants. X marks the spot but staring at the gorse
I had so totally failed to map it. What I had thought
of as an easily circumambulated patch was a sick
and dizzy green and yellow sea stretching on forever.
I crouched down at the edge of one of the ghost
ponds. The bare ground underneath the bushes was
mulched with all types of detritus excrement an old
feed bag baling twine a sheep skeleton picked or
weathered clean scatter of loose teeth pink bobble
hat fallen out of someone's pack another walker had
picked it up and stuck it on the gorse opened out like
a monstrous mutant flower. The phone was pink
too you got me to bid on it by saying pink stuff went
for cheaper still cost a fair whack and you haven't
reimbursed me yet BTW. It seemed improbable some
gleam of metal or smashed glass would reveal its
whereabouts. I could have spent more money hiring
a metal detector but the ground would be rich in
further distractions chucked ring pulls old tins a
broken walking pole any unexploded WW2 ordnance
ditched by planes heading home after bombing
London or laid deliberately as the Downs were trans-
formed into a minefield against anticipated invasion,
you said. If the enemy had managed to cut through
the massive rolls of barbed wire that blocked the
beaches subdued the coastal settlements and started
inland towards the capital all the roads and railways
would have been blown up and so the hills would
have been the only way left. Not much of an obstacle

in themselves but wired and mined at strategic and
random points to spread fear and confusion among
soldiers who whatever poisonous political ideas they
had been indoctrinated with remained in the majority hapless teenagers. I remember you looked at us
then as if expecting to be challenged but none of
us did. But of course that never happened so after
the war it took years to find and remove the mines.
I'm saying this as part of general housekeeping
health and safety gone mad ha ha but I did once find
an intact grenade poking about so if you ever see
something you think looks like a bomb

Of course Angela would have had no problem retrieving the phone. The denouement of that freaky
scene up at the ponds would have been etched onto
her brainbox crystal clear. She would recollect
exactly where she had been standing and netball
captain's muscle memory would have retained a
precise idea of how far she could throw. She could
have come up here at any point in the past ten days,
armed with thick clothing and something to hack
her way through the gorse, and she could have gone
in there and got the phone out with a minimum of
fuss. Take out the memory card and drop the phone
into a small electricals recycling bin all those rare
earth metals kids halfway around the world were
going to have the fun of retrieving or seal the whole
thing inside a freezer bag and keep it at the back
of a drawer as a memento of her most righteous anger.
Not like I could have any idea of what might have
been inside her head when she climbed the hill again.
Simmering hatred or had she calmed down. Perish

the thought might she even be seeing the funny side. Roy's decision to go sky-clad demonstrating the extent to which he had run out of options. Not that he'd ever felt inhibited about taking off his clothes. He enjoyed being naked. Lucky him. Compensated for his lack of a silver tongue. Why I tolerated him as my roomie if he'd blethered on like anybody's business he would have been out on his ear. Why had we ever become friends when you analysed it was it just a question of mutual need and if so what had we seen in each other had I just thought this guy has got something I can use and had he felt the same about me? As for Angela playing the beautiful slightly troubled young woman not entirely sure what was good for her don't take it the wrong way if I say she's grown up a lot. Licorice certainly won't be taking any credit. Whenever Angie's name crops up it's in a studiedly neutral tone. I have totally failed to see the funny side of her working that big deliberate bloody handprint into my car. At one point I was feeling like she'd hexed me. Thanks to you Ange I no longer feel I have a car. For the umpteenth time can I just get me to shut up this is fucking idiotic

Whenever Angela had come back I'm guessing that you would have followed the route I had to today, getting the bus along to just opposite where the road to the village turns off and then madly ducking across the dual carriageway through streams of traffic at a designated pedestrian crossing I'd never noticed in all the times I'd driven past. Up that road past the wastewater treatment plant to the hollow where Nan's remains rest somewhere underneath the tarmac and the chalk. The track to the left leading up to the windmill. The path to the right in the direction of the ponds. The trees here are different. Everything is different. I shouldn't even be trying to imagine the scene we were never going to shoot it but here it is couched entirely in terms of old horror films. Nan is dragged out of the dark cellar where she's been kept while the community decided on her fate. A cord binds her arms to her sides clad as a penitent in only her off-white shift she shakes the hair away from her face and appears dazed she can't stop blinking at the sun. And would her eyes be red with weeping would she stand meekly nodding her head to confirm the justice of the sentence that is about to be carried out or would she rant and curse everyone calling down her bitter vengeance on all future generations of villagers with their silent disapproving faces a special mention for the local bigwigs by whose justice she had been so consummately failed. Or would she have been so completely out of it wishing herself anywhere but here none of this is real I am dreaming in my own bed I am asleep under the hawthorn up on the hill and all these images and thoughts are not my own why are they tormenting me another's thoughts have broken into my head. He is not here thank my unlucky stars for that. What is the moment of death actually like? Flashes of light and ringing or hissing in the ears intense mental confusion the loss of all power of what's described here as logical thought quickly followed by unconsciousness you hope. Struggling and convulsions continue. As her nervous system is so rudely interrupted Nan loses control of her bowels and bladder too a final indignity that at least she would not have been aware of. Though the heart can keep beating for several minutes after respiration has stopped. Eyes prominent the skin of her face livid or dusky or engorged depending on how the ligature had compressed the blood vessels in her neck. So Angela when you reached the gorse bushes were you worried that if you crawled into them to retrieve the phone you would be seen by people coming along the path dog walkers at any rate because it's not like runners ever look at what isn't in front of them. Or did you just think if anyone asks me what I am doing I can explain I had an argument with ma boy up here the other day and threw my phone into these bushes. That is the kind of thing they would accept from the ditsy girl they'd be reading me as. Like I didn't want that tosser ever bothering me again and then once I got home I thought about all the other shit that was on there. What am I like ha ha ha ha. It's cheaper and easier to block him. What looks like blonde human hair caught on the prickles. Ripped from someone's scalp as they pushed their way through. Yellow as among the yellow flowers. Licorice never had Ange in a blonde wig and this is real hair, not synthetic. You can usually tell by touch and if you're not sure put a match to it the smell is an instant giveaway

What's this Pete peace offering of course I know it's not your favourite food but there's a fillet of rock salmon bit of haddock you can have whichever you prefer chips in that big container and nuke green mushy peas don't know if you like those Licorice if not I'll eat them all sachets of salt pepper vinegar ketchup brown sauce mayonnaise tried to think of everything brought my own plates and cutlery so not leaving you any washing up can I come in. We have to talk was what I didn't say. Bottle of nice French white ooh look I know you have mugs. Can I pour you some? Let's tuck in before this grub goes cold. Sitting across her kitchen table among all the things I'd come to be familiar with I couldn't but feel something had changed at the same time I didn't want to be obviously looking around or even like I was trying really hard not to because she would pick it up she had radar like a bat so I concentrated on eating and behaving like I had no idea anything was different. The notebooks were gone. The draining board was cleared of paints and dust. Where was her log book? She'd probably just filed everything away in her bedroom for safer keeping. I filled up the mugs because to fill them partway would have seemed mean. Licorice unwrapped the piece of haddock onto her plate sawed through the batter and started flaking off tiny bits of fish. Like she was expecting there to be bones. I didn't say anything

Licorice is drinking her mug of wine like it's lemonade steadily sucking it down without coughing or spluttering. I've never seen her drink like this. A little more colour in her cheeks her eyes brightening it is the first time in quite a few days she is coming back into focus. I pour the rest of the bottle into her mug but for the moment she doesn't touch it. What have you been up to today Pete? Oh various chores. Pulling stuff together for tomorrow. Went to the station to buy my weekly season more than a hundred quid but worth it since I'll be travelling up to London every day. Congratulations. What is it you're doing again exactly? Oh you know what these things are like won't find out the finer details until I get there I tried to joke. Well you deserve it. You've been very patient. No one deserves stuff Licorice and I would never say patience was my middle name I was lucky a guy I knew needed a fourth assistant director and I got a rep how well deserved you're in a position to judge as a safe pair of hands. A quite uncharacteristic outbreak of humility on my part as I shovelled in the largest forkful of mushy peas. Have some of these chips Licorice before I eat them all. She smiled and put one into her mouth but the action of chewing it seemed to go on forever

Found myself back in the village pub today. Really. Whatever were you doing there? Bit more of a reccy round some of the twittens and backyards there's not so many kids around now all the schools are back so quieter and easier to have a snoop. Oh and did you find what you were looking for I think you were wasting your time there's no more filming to be done anything else would be very soggy seconds. Another sip of wine and you are staring at me like you know exactly how good a liar I am. Maybe this'll interest you Licorice. The people from the windmill were in the pub. Back from their six weeks on a remote Greek island it transpires. Of course I had no idea who they were when they came in I was just nursing my pint and a packet of crisps but all became clear once the landlord started in with the bants. Did they recognise you Pete what are they like? Oh white middle-aged and prosperous who'd have thought. She has long dark hair in a ponytail he hasn't much at all and she was wearing a fancy pair of glasses not reacting as fast as they should to changing light because she stumbled and almost fell down those two steps if you remember into the bar. The wanderers return was what the landlord had actually said. Been hitting the old ouzo Lucy? Never been tempted by ouzo, Ben, because I don't like the taste of liquorice. Luckily the wine was so good; they've got grapes on the island that aren't grown anywhere else. After a couple of weeks we were starting to believe the brochure hype. So great being away from work am I rubbing that in enough? Six weeks' digital detox in effect but blimey is everything piled up to deal with now. Welcome to my world. So how are your good lady and the kids? Oh you know I keep telling them they mustn't grumble. Do they listen? You're both looking very well at any rate what can I get you

Nicely tanned from their six weeks in the sun, wearing sensible country clothes *you* might be able to classify as more expensive than they looked. A black and white springer spaniel lolling round their feet affectionate alert intelligent Jasper's been missing you the landlord remarked his treats too I reckon can he have his usual. We've missed him too missus miller replied can't wait to take him out for a proper long walk. Too much else to do today and we wanted to come down and see you of course but tomorrow. They were having to put up with being joshed about when exactly their windmill was going to be finished and get some corn ground in it. How did they take that? Like they was used to it smiled politely and drank up their beer then headed off over the village green with Jasper in tow. Jasper Licorice said what a name for a dog. She replaced her knife and fork on the plate from which she had eaten precisely half the fish and steepled her fingers. What type of dog is Jasper again? You nod gravely and take another mouthful of wine. Almost the inverse of that fierce dog guarding the tailpole in the Luttrell Psalter he has a heavy collar broad snout pricked-up ears and a curled tail. Mmm. I think Licorice you are definitely drunk. They didn't say anything about my drawings? Licorice why would they in the course of a conversation like that

Well they obviously haven't been gagging to get in touch with us my contact details were on every note I posted through the door and I haven't heard a peep Licorice. So they're mulling it over. Or they haven't had the chance to think it through yet. If I could talk to them before they make up their minds if I apologise for putting so much paper through their door if I can involve them in what for lack of a better word shall we call our vision Pete you know some kind of charm offensive if I can muster the energy she shrugged. Explain what we are trying to achieve. Flatter them. You know what hobbyists are like express interest in their project ask them about the materials and techniques they used I wouldn't even have to fake my interest in their answers. Might not mention the zoetrope they could be uneasy at the idea of their home spinning round like a top. She giggled then splaying her fingers in front of her face. Cup of tea if you like. No thanks Licorice I'll finish this. She giggled again at least I assumed that was going on head pillowed on her arms crossed on the table shoulders shaking through her thin stripy jumper black and pink did that count as a departure from her usual colour scheme. When she raised her head there was moisture on her right cheek probably just drops of spilt wine from the table but it hit me then I had never seen her cry and this was did it have to pop into my mind what she would look like if she started melting

Take me up to the windmill in the morning Pete. Licorice I'm starting my new job. Oh you know what these things are like on the first day you said yourself that you're not sure yet what you'll be doing it's just going to be milling around doing paperwork and sorting out preliminary schedules. She took another mouthful of wine. Licorice I'm going to have to do all that at some stage my not being there tomorrow doesn't mean I'll get out of filling forms and how as a lowly fourth assistant director can I swap any places that clash in the schedules if I'm not actually on the spot? I am listening to you Pete and that's all true but I've got to go up to the windmill tomorrow morning and talk to them. We've nearly missed the boat on this well whose fault is that I bit my tongue and I can't go up there all by myself Pete on the bus I just can't. I can't go up to the door and knock they might not be there in any case if we take your car at least we'll have somewhere to sit and wait rather than crouching under the trees forecast is sixty percent chance of precipitation I've just checked. You're my partner my co-director half this film is yours remember? You owe

it to me Pete and to yourself too don't you think?
Do you think it's really going to make all that much
difference in your new job if you miss the first day

At least you've got something of your mojo back but
what timing and how had I got myself into a position
where I couldn't walk away. If I had been living
somewhere else I might have felt able to give the film
up as a bad job but in the same house as her it was
difficult to get her out of my thoughts. I was always
thinking what is she doing down below and why
is she so quiet. No way was I taking my car. Very expensive to hire one at the last minute the limited
choice of available vehicles meant I ended up with a
far dearer model than I had intended. When I picked
her up at 8.15 she was standing on the pavement
wearing sunglasses and holding a big bag once upon
a time I would have quipped she was channelling
the wary film star but now I just opened the car door
barely grunting hi. I've brought a couple of hi-vis
jackets taking a leaf out of your book Pete she said.
I could have pointed out that hi-vis jackets didn't
really fit with the car I was driving today and I should
definitely not be driving it up this steep lane not
trying to park on a rough unmade verge under the
trees because even though hire included a damage
waiver I very much doubted if anything more than
dropped crumbs or a smidge of birdshit would be
covered. They had my credit card details. How much
deeper in debt would I be this evening thanks to this
sleek black monster with all the sorts of gadgets I had
no idea how to use? I feel like your chauffeur Licorice.
Not meant to make her laugh I was expressing my

frustration. So let me pour you some coffee Pete.
Oh sorry yes I should have remembered you're a flat
white man. She sneezed twice. Don't think I've finally
caught Roy's cold that magic tree must be giving me
hay fever I am definitely more sensitive to chemicals
than I used to be it doesn't affect you Pete? No. I
don't get hay fever. I could feel her looking at me but
gazed straight ahead up the lane. If she just thought
I should be at her beck and call evidently there was
nothing else in my life worth getting on with. I could
have gone on holiday this summer rather than get
involved with her film. Or saved that leftover funding
for a project that had some prospect of success

What part of a six weeks' digital detox Licorice
do you not understand? The millers never responded
to the alerts on their phones they never saw the
footage generated by their security camera they never
even thought about entering our biometric details
into their database. That huge pile of your drawings
on their mat would have come as a complete shock
on their return. Do bear in mind Pete that I'm just
throwing ideas at you here if anything comes across
as too weird or if there's something you think you
might agree with then feel free to shout out. There
were quite a few occasions I was here on my own
and of course I came up here with Angie the day we
were all in the pub and she had got herself into such
a state. Peak sad if you know what I mean mooning
after that wretched Roy. She reached out to me. I just
let her talk. Never thought of myself as cut out to be
anyone's confidante but at the time. You stopped,
obviously finding this difficult. Maybe if I hadn't let

her talk that day maybe if I hadn't let her feel she could trust me then she would never have been so angry. So easy with hindsight isn't it Pete? When you can see where things went wrong. Why are you asking Licorice you want to hear what I would have done if Angela had reached out to me? Just thought that didn't say it you are gazing at me and to punctuate the silence I shrug and shake my head. Change of tack. So your visiting the pub yesterday Pete has also reminded me how that passage leading down to the loos struck me at the time as our perfect interior you don't recall maybe the gents was in the opposite direction take the posters off the walls suspend sacking over the light switches locked doors anything else giving the game away. The stone floor was right. So fucking cold. Bit of straw to up the ambience I'll clean so thoroughly afterwards it'll be cleaner than it was before boobed completely saying that to the landlady the look she gave me was who are you strange foreign woman to implicitly criticise anything I do or ha ha don't. Why I didn't tell you at the time. We all had other things on our minds

Treacherous image of a narrow shadowy passage with a ceiling not so low Thomas would have to bend his head hair the colour of a bright damp conker and Nan in her fourteenth century blue woollen dress and red cloak where she has come in out of the rain pressed into his arms. They are kissing passionately and in the background distorted sounds of a baby crying wa wa wa wa wa leave it leave it it won't come to harm. Nan's hands clasped Thomas round his middle so small no her fingernails are not dirty

119

she always keeps them very clean clatter bang
ouch Nan's left shoulder scraping the stone wall each
time he thrusts his prick up inside of her hoarse
heavy breathing you revolting beasts continence is
unknown to you Nan plucks at his shirt then with
increasing urgency. Stop it you stop. She's trying to
wriggle away but she's jammed against the wall and
the little she can move her hips is speeding up his
climax. Both hands now. You promised you'd stop.
Thomas groans give a final heave and withdraws. A
bit on the late side his penis is sticky already small
and flaccid he parries her hands searching for it
to check stuffs it hastily back under whatever he's
wearing. Moves his right hand back up to her cunt
warm wiry scrape of her pubic hair slippery with
cum and her own fluids best way to distract her from
his failure she's going to be mad as hell if she finds
out. Spilt on the floor mine own heart's root. Lost
in the dirt under our feet. My lambkin. Has he fooled
her? Soft groans and moans she shudders and he
laughs catching her around the waist and pulls her
to him murmuring endearments thick yellow hair
dishevelled over her shoulders where her damp red
hood has fallen back her breasts swollen globes with
hard oozing nipples he loves the feel of them like
this smelling incredibly of warm cream. He would
really like to suckle her but that's just going to
bring her mind back to the baby which has stopped
crying for now. For a moment she is quiet in his arms
and he thinks he's got away with it. Then she stirs
and starts to pummel at his chest. You think I'm
stupid. You think I am that thick

The leaves we can see from the car are covered with tar spots disease or the mark of some stage in the life cycle of an insect guest they remind me of pips on the face of a die except they're not regularly arranged. Splatter of molten tar on the road only on the hottest of days smell of petrol and boiled sweets spots on my grandfather's hands patience is hardly a spectator sport young man what's your favourite game Licorice had asked me as we were sat there waiting for them to show I dunno. Cluedo? Yes that's okay did you ever see the dreadful movie? No. Is Miss Scarlet named for Scarlett O'Hara do you think? I have no fucking idea. It's my fault you're in such a bad temper Pete. Literally Licorice it is just everything today. Well once I've talked to them you can take me back home it's still quite early maybe you'll get up to London today after all. Whatever Licorice. Mister and missus miller are coming down the lane with Jasper their dog bounding ahead of them. Looking pretty cheerful but why not; they can congratulate themselves on having escaped that miserable English August. Such a cluster of rain events defo the result of anthropogenic global warming but look on the bright side at least we're not facing a hosepipe ban next year when we want to get the garden up and running. Missus miller reaches forward and gets the dog to sit while she rubs its ears hardly surprising Jasper's antsy after rotting in kennels for six weeks her husband is putting his oar in about dog management but she shrugs and feeds the dog a biscuit without looking up at him. Just a casual glance registering the unfamiliar car but it's the kind of car someone visiting their neighbours might have and though it seems a

little odd it's parked on the rough verge the two
of us sitting inside merit no more comprehensive
second glance. You were right about the jackets being
camouflage said Licorice but why wasn't she stirring
herself here's your golden opportunity to ask them
all those questions you've just been going through
with me. They're taking the dog for a long walk
they're not going to be back for ages do you want to
wait? For fuck's sake! I couldn't believe she bottled
it. Grasped the door handle like she was going to get
out of the car and then couldn't. Mister and missus
and Jasper have already disappeared down the lane.
Licorice! I grabbed her shoulders but she was so
scarily still I thought she must be having some kind
of momentary absence fit. Her hands were on her
lap. Your hands are freezing. Which of these fucking
buttons works the heater. She stirred and smiled
faintly then reached into her pocket and pulled out
a carefully folded brown paper bag. Breathed into
it and then sucked the air back out slowly into her
cheeks. She did this a few times. I didn't trust myself
to say anything. I'm not completely starving myself
of oxygen Pete. I'll catch them on their way back
home when the dog is tired it will be much easier to
talk to them

Was it the thought of having to introduce yourself
that led to that failure of nerve? Hi there I'm Licorice
shake your hand or would you have introduced
yourself by your birth name which I still don't know.
Missus miller could be exactly your age she's not
tall either both of you gather your long dark hair back
in a ponytail and is this what is freaking you out

making you so much more aware of the unbridgeable gap between your life and theirs? A strong conviction that the millers are not going to welcome your intervention with open arms they are not going to say we've been oh so curious about who could have put those amazing pictures through our door! Did you really want them back? What a pity.... Maybe we could keep a few to hang up on our living room walls. You've caught a great sense of the atmosphere we particularly like those drawings of the windmill's interior. Is it creepy to think that you've been observing us all this time? No you got those pictures off the internet and the old postcard yes those old postcards are great we think of them as windows back into a different world

No all the drawings she had put through the door would have been muddled up with every other bit of crap on the mat and if rain had leaked in too then the ink would have got well and truly splotched. When mister and missus returned from their six weeks' digital detox their first action would have been to go eeuggh we'll have to get a sticker requesting no junk mail or circulars and in heaven's name why are all these tightly folded bits of paper here forsooth? They look like a cartoon but we have no idea of running order. What do they show? Detailed sketches of street furniture in the village the posting box the noticeboard low flint walls the old K6 phonebox that never works. Tug of war and a man dressed as a bear at the village fete. Images of the road with blurred cars passing at the foot of our lane. Plastic roses in a vase on a tiled sill. Drawings of the pub no way is that us standing at the bar? The village green in the direction of the playground. A-board strung with a mesh of wire diamonds blank of grabby headlines for a change outside the shop. The twitten between the old cottages pipes leaking lichen dark twisty uneven dig up those paving stones. Several drawings of a naked young couple fucking in a series of positions. A woman hanging from a tree with a bag over her head bare legs dangling her hands tied behind her back. A woman with long black hair lying on the grass by the pond, ear pressed to the ground. More of her spreadeagled with piles of chalk on top of her hands and feet. One where just her head is emerging from the ground. And that expression? I don't want to look at them any more. Well we can recycle them Lucy. Or would you rather feed them to the stove? Let's burn them. I don't want them lying around. Scatter their atoms in smoke to the four winds

Weren't the acoustics of this all-wooden building why we wanted to get in here in the first place? Okay I can dangle my phone through the letter box to record whatever sounds there are not as elaborate as our original plan but we must cut our coat according to our cloth. Should have thought of that before. Like you said they're bound to be ages. Of course I won't drop my phone and right now I don't care about the fucking camera. If you do Pete then I'll go up there on my own and you can stop here and wait for me. Have the engine running in case we need to make a quick getaway ha ha ha. Licorice strange slight figure carrying a plastic bag look at you disappearing up the lane and you still haven't taken off the hi-vis jacket with that on you certainly look like you've come to fix something. All in black with this bright dayglo you walk as if impatient to be somewhere else. Get inside the mill if you think you can I wouldn't be surprised if advanced lockpicking does feature in your skill set. Always one of your wrinkles to draw the space re-enclosed after all this time. Indeed the more I think about it the more I'm convinced that's what you really intend to do. The drawings you posted through the door still there as ghosts fucking spells on paper just as much as the eddies of information you invited us to immerse ourselves in. Such a fast worker of course you have paper and ink with you. No longer worrying about the one Angela picked up and took away you could redo the whole lot at top speed because they are perfectly clear in your mind. And if you are drawing inside the windmill you can stick up each sheet as it's done you have blu tack magic tape a good supply of drawing pins in your bag. The stutter of whatever narrative you have plumped for unfurls on the walls. Maybe you are applying the drawings in several tiers so the imaginary viewer's eye can spiral through them or for fuck's sake they can do their own jumpcuts through the various loops

I imagine you sitting with your legs crossed on the floor alternatively you might be kneeling bum well back on your heels with your bare feet stretched out behind you soles uppermost. I'm older than you Pete. I get aches and pains. But if I keep on sitting like this and getting up and down off the floor every day then I'm always barring a terrible unforeseen life-changing accident ha ha ha going to be able to do so. You might bend forward slowly until the weight of your torso rested along your thighs and you could touch the floor with your forehead, arms extended in front of you on the bare boards. New pine. Or had they been stained to resemble something else. The curves of your spine visible through the black T-shirt. Great way of uncranking my back you should try it some time. Lying there meditating your phone switched to do not disturb. I don't like answering it Pete. If you want to call, text me first so I know it's you. Where are you? I had texted but nothing back. What do you want me to do? didn't work either. I tried calling her then but as I thought straight to unavailable. Could be the network's dodgy coverage. Checking for wifi brought up a list of silly names, all locked. *Windy* down there at the bottom feeble one bar signal if I follow you into the mill odds are we would find the password written down within three metres of the hub such a strange thought that via this route all the security footage showing us had been uploaded and then vanished in the ether. Is the mill furnished with choice antiques from distant lands glowing scarlet and orange patterned rugs sexy rosewood bureaux a pair of those big blue and white chinoiserie vases people keep walking sticks and umbrellas in because what the fuck else can you do with them? The other option I'm considering, Licorice had said, is completely kitted out from Ikea all the beds tables chairs storage for clothes bright pictures in beechwood frames house plants in those galvanised metal troughs like half the holiday lets in the world. Except they're never going to get enough light through those tiny windows do you reckon they

have some sophisticated ambient lighting system
in there Pete? Controlled by another little robot
simulated daylight courtesy of the solar panels
on the roof making visible the brand new dust.
Rubbings off the building materials. However many
months of just the millers' skin cells and stray hairs.
You'll be adding a few of your own. Feeling your
presence ripple and disturb the space. Are there even
spiders in there yet. All the angles and intersections
of the building raw and pristine

What kinds of timber would traditionally have been
deployed where? Strong durable oak would have
been top choice for the main framework and drive
shafts. Historically elm cheaper lighter though not
as long-lasting would have been second option for the
frame. Baltic pine for the weatherboarding. Licorice
laughs. After the discovery of the new world pitch
pine which provides very long strong and to some
degree rot-resistant timber might have been used for
the sweeps. In Nan's day the sweeps would have been
covered with sailcloth not the intricate system of
adjustable shutters developed later. Metal was rarely
used. The teeth of the geared wheels regulating
the mill's interior mechanisms would be formed
of apple pear or hornbeam because these woods
have a fine grain and are relatively free of knots.
Wooden treenails driven into pre-drilled holes hold
the timbers in place but the structure's resistance
to shear force depends on the quality of its mortise
tenon dovetail and double bird's mouth joints. No the
sweeps of the mill turn anti-clockwise. Generating
messages. One windmill down by the shore was

used by smugglers whichever tilt of the sweeps sending a coded instruction to boats out at sea. For a birth a wedding or in celebration of some great national event each idle mill would be positioned with one sweep approaching (that's to the left as you're looking at the mill) the perpendicular. About to *almost* touch the ground. Anticipating a happy future. Conversely if the mill is at rest with a sweep just leaving the perpendicular it betokens mourning for someone or something that has recently gone away. Like giant semaphore. Broadcasting to quite a distance. Even if Nan and Thomas had never been taught their alphabet they would have made sense of *these* messages. And isn't it interesting, you add, that although the energy that powers the sweeps comes from the sky their touchstone the point of reference where humans read them as expressing meaning is the earth? Your scanty precious sacred dirt Pete painstakingly manured with sheep dung to boost its flagging yields. The lord's monopoly meant all grain grown in the local area had to be milled here hoisted up to the top of this wooden building trickling or streaming down the chute depending on how hard the wind is blowing

Wood has a much lower mass than many other construction materials even small amounts of energy cause it to vibrate surely when they built this facsimile windmill they would have put in really good soundproofing I mean who wants to live in a building that sighs and groans whenever the wind blows? Thermal insulation just as critical in this exposed spot: the more passive the building the more power

generated by these sweeps should they ever turn
will flow directly into the grid. They could have used
that fabulous golden German stuff that looks like a
survival blanket. Back in Licorice's kitchen is a pile
of offcuts I'm not throwing them away Pete believe it
or not this malarkey costs hundreds of pounds a roll.
Cloth of gold. Imagine the field of the cloth of gold all
draped with this. Imagine a cloak made out of it wd
kp u v wrm. Wrapping the inside of the building and
then I guess a stud wall and plasterboard to form
the skin of the room? Or they could have used sheep's
wool another eco-friendly option though its bulk
would have added a few cm to the insulating layer and
in a skinny predetermined space like the windmill
they would surely want to maximise the interior.
Needs to be properly fire-retardant too, especially in
a wooden structure that could go up like a torch

The tailpole is part of the same structure as the
spindly steps leading up to the body of the mill. I think
of Licorice's words about the fantackle if it had been
in place this structure could automatically attune
itself to the wind. Back in Nan's day the miller
would have had to adjust the post mill manually by
pushing the tailpole around until the sweeps were
aligned into the wind at the most productive angle.
A gruelling task even if the mill was smaller and
lighter in those days. The lower end of the tailpole is
fitted into a circular metal groove in the grass. So
to get the mill working the first thing to do is to estab-
lish the direction of the wind and then shove the
tailpole round so the body of the mill turns until the
wind hits the edge of the sweeps. I lick my finger

raise my arm above my head and close my eyes. Licorice would laugh if she saw me now. West. East. Is there any wind at all? *O westron wynde when wilt thou blow the small rain down can rain Cryste, if my love was in my arms and I in my bedde again!* The dual carriageway in the valley below runs north to south. The track to the east of the windmill is almost parallel to it: woods on the far side mean the windmill doesn't get the morning sun until it has lost every tinge of pink. From the west fiery reds and yellows as the sun appears to sink into the sea. Nothing to obstruct the glorious late afternoon light pouring through those tiny windows colouring every little bit of the interior. Mister scrolling and sighing through his emails Jasper's hackles rise has he smelt a rat

We'll get something great out of this yet never you fear. Your Aeolian harps Licorice; happen we should construct them after all. Remember when you made the first one I said the sound of them up on the hills would scare me shitless? That's why you never placed the harp in your kitchen window to conjure whatever sweet sounds from the breeze in our backyard. I've come to feel it was a pity. I was wrong Licorice. *Mea culpa* works like a charm. Slumped in the car after the millers have disappeared down the lane, you turn to look at me. My reaction back then showed how your idea really hit a nerve: instead of moaning on at you I should have thought why exactly am I feeling this way? Deep-seated worries probed a fucking biopsy of anxiety put it right up under the magnifying lens try to detect a pattern even if it gets you no nearer to solving the root cause. Licorice throws back her head and laughs. I join in the hilarity. Is it cathartic, signalling a release of tension? You tell me Pete she says. I'm thinking more than ever that I should have stuck to comedy

I line myself up about three quarters of the way along the tailpole and shove with all the strength I possess. Even harder than it looks but that's because it's new and never been moved before if I just keep pushing it will probably start to budge. Faulty logic. The whole contraption could be braked somewhere inside the mill and I wouldn't have a clue. Try it the other way and it gives a couple of cm but realistically that is back to square one I'm cashing in the illusion of gain my efforts have bought. Crap. This is making me feel dizzy sick blood pounding in my ears I've never aspired to be particularly fit or strong never spent hours in the gym doing bench press and all the other kind of shit my former roomie did. Building up his muscles. I shut my eyes and think for a moment if I can just imagine him standing beside me. Come on Roy come on my Charles Atlas buddy give me a hand now why wouldn't you to absolutely no avail

The door at the top of the steps is firmly locked. I spot the cam but I'm not stepping backwards on this narrow platform to wave hello. How the fuck did I ever entertain the thought that this door might have open-sesamed for Licorice? Well maybe the millers left it on the latch but in the very unlikely event of that happening she wouldn't be shutting the door behind her would she? Perhaps she hasn't noticed it has closed trapping her. Reclaimed hardwood deadens the impact of my fists and if there's an acoustic panel on the back Licorice is never going to hear me. I'm never going to hear her inside of there either. She could be screaming at the top of her voice and I wouldn't know. How likely is that Licorice please answer me. Even if you're engrossed in drawing or tracking whatever sounds you perceive around you you're surely glancing at the security display from time to time to check whether the millers are coming back

Turning round abruptly from the door wasn't a great idea. The view from the top of the steps falls away much further than to the solid ground where the steps begin. Right to the bottom of the valley with the railway and the dual carriageway even further down all the way to the sea. The intersecting curves of the hills form temporary new horizons. I feel giddy and have to sit down. Because it's one thing looking at the horizon like it divides the earth from the sky quite another when you're gazing down on it as a constantly extending field of operation. Nowhere to stop. It shifts. Ribboning. No reason to stop. Patterns of trees. Cloud shadows. The rush of cars speeding on straight through. Birds of the Downs one of Licorice's many lists herring gull corn bunting kestrel magpie pheasant crows ravens I think she said skylark yellowhammer. Oh look there goes one down the lane! Fabulous colour. Did you get it Pete? Wood pigeons in the trees where the car is parked it's been over an hour

Maybe she never even tried to get into the windmill. If she'd already decided not to when she left the car then she deliberately blindsided me but I don't know for certain and therefore I can't act as if I do. If she kept going straight past the windmill the track would take her across a large open field through a gate into a wood and gradually down across the dual carriageway and the railway via the high concrete span used by cars as well. Shadowing the railway to the station and for a moment I imagine you gazing up at the departure boards there is at least one port and an airport among the potential destinations what might prompt you to make any kind of decision? Licorice! Who am I kidding when did you ever listen to me? You didn't have to stick to that track there were footpaths spidering off in different directions or you might have plumped for any point on the horizon and be walking steadily towards it. Once you'd taken off your hi-vis jacket, folding it neatly to stow away under a bush. But why would you do that and leave me to stew in my own juice? She must know, mustn't she, that I can't leave here without knowing what has happened to her. At some point the millers are coming back and what the fuck am I going to say? My friend has vanished into thin air. So report her disappearance to the police. Licorice I'm bored with waiting. Where are you girl? Time to go home

Author's acknowledgements
My thanks to everyone at Book Works. James Langdon
for his design. Paul Holman, Harriet Holman Penney,
Marius Holman Penney, Jeff Noon, Katrina Palmer, Jo Penney
and Stef Penney for being early readers. Shuhong Jiang,
Bob Lewis, Isabel Smith and Gloria Stuart Hutcheson for
conversations that dripped intravenously into *Licorice*.
Harry Gilonis and Woodrow Phoenix for answering questions.

Licorice
by Bridget Penney
Interstices No. 1

Published and distributed by Book Works, London
© Bridget Penney, 2020

ISBN 978 1 912570 05 8

Commissioning editor: Bridget Penney
Proofread by Jenny Fisher
Designed by James Langdon
Typeset in Triptych by Stefan Ellmer
Cover lettering by Sun Young Oh
Printed by die Keure, Bruges

Book Works
19 Holywell Row, London EC2A 4JB
www.bookworks.org.uk
Tel. +44 (0)20 7247 2203

Book Works is funded by Arts Council England